In honor of good people everywhere.
Madelyn S Palmer

Elinore's Choice

Madelyn S. Palmer

Order this book online at www.trafford.com
or email orders@trafford.com

Most Trafford titles are also available at major online book retailers.

Printed in the United States of America.

ISBN: 978-1-4669-9275-7 (sc)
ISBN: 978-1-4669-9274-0 (e)

Trafford rev. 05/02/2013

 www.trafford.com

North America & international
toll-free: 1 888 232 4444 (USA & Canada)
phone: 250 383 6864 ♦ fax: 812 355 4082

CHAPTER 1

The Test at Rimrock Island

I t was shortly before sunrise, and Elinore sat next to her father in the shadows of the canopied royal stand. She looked out at Rimrock Island where it lay in the partly sheltered bay of the coastline. This was the fourteenth suitor (or was it the fifteenth?) this month to attempt to pass the test her father required for her hand in marriage. This man was the son of some royalty from Persia. Or was it Arabia? She wished she had brought a book to read.

Her father arose, and the five subjects standing around to witness the event seemed to wake up a little.

"My People of Sterling," King Louis began. Even he doesn't sound enthusiastic anymore, Elinore thought. "We are gathered here to witness the historic attempt, ah-hem, event of Prince Abram of ah, um, Sahaja, to take The Test to win the hand of my daughter in marriage." The king paused, and nudged his daughter with his foot. She was jerked from her reverie just in time to flash her typical court smile for the group. He then turned to the suitor waiting in readiness on his horse beside the stand. "You understand the rules?"

The suitor looked over at Elinore, squared his shoulders, and smiled confidently. "Yes!" he affirmed, his voice deep and rich, and with a colorful lilting accent. "I am ready."

The king looked up at the sky. The first orange colors of dawn were spilling across the horizon, and starting to light the hills behind the group gathered on the beach. All eyes were glued to where sky met sea as the sky grew brighter and brighter. Then in the center of the brightest area, a sliver of the golden sun appeared, spilling its rays onto the coastline watchers.

"Now!" said the king, raising his voice slightly for the benefit of his audience. "Let the test begin."

Prince Abram spurred his horse and it leaped forward, slithered down a short muddy slope toward the beach, pounded across the strip of sand, and plunged into the waves dashing onto the shore. Horse and rider could be seen intermittently between upheavals of the waves, growing smaller and looking increasingly vulnerable in the powerful sea. Then suddenly they were there, rider leading his horse between the boulders strewn upon Rimrock's shore, and up into the trees. Then they were gone. The villagers comprising the audience began to disperse.

"Well, Elinore," said her father, turning to her. "I'll be giving audience again today if you should need me. Otherwise, I'll bring you and Celia some dinner when I return." He kissed her forehead, climbed into his carriage, yawned, then began sorting through papers as it rolled away.

"He has little enough time to get things done as it is," commented Elinore to her attendant, Celia, as she watched him depart. "If only for his sake, I hope one of these suitors will hurry up and pass The Test, so he won't have to waste so much time away from court matters." She sighed and turned back to face the front of the stand.

One of the villagers was standing by his horse and wagon in front of her, holding his hat respectfully in his hand. "Good day to you, Princess," he grinned cheerfully.

"Good morning to you, Robert of Danforth," she returned with a warm smile. He was one of the few villagers who faithfully attended the suitor contests. "Where are you off to today?"

"I'm going to the market in Norton to trade with the mountain people. I hear their furs are some of the best. Is there anything you would like me to look for?"

Elinore thought for a moment. "I think I would like to get my father a fur for a warm hunting cap. Something soft, and with a bluish or white color to it." She opened her purse and withdrew some coins for him.

Robert laughed. "And nothing for you, My Lady?"

She shook her head. "I don't need anything, Robert. Really!"

"Very well, Princess," he said, winking at Celia, who winked back. "I will bring you the best fur for a hunting cap that there is." He turned toward his horse, and clicked his tongue. "Come, Bart. We have a trip to make this day." He tipped his hat to the two ladies, climbed up into the wagon, slapped the horse's reins smartly and drove away, whistling a merry tune.

"Well, Celia. It looks as though we have another day at the beach. What exciting activities are offered us today?"

Celia put her hands on her hips. "And what about your lessons, My Lady?"

Elinore waved her hand. "I can do those in minutes. What else is to be done?"

Celia held up a basket of mending. "The children's clothes are in a sorry state, My Lady. I'm afraid they will demand much of the day to repair."

"You can stop talking so formally, Celia," Elinore laughed. "Father isn't around to hear you anyway." Elinore moved her chair aside, sat down on the floor of the stand at Celia's feet, reached into the basket and pulled out a pair of stockings. "I am ready for my stitchery lesson, Madam. Where wouldst thou have me begin?"

Celia drew an extra needle from a small bag on her lap, and sorted through the basket until she found a ball of yarn of the right color. "Thread your needle, My Lady. Then find two stones the right size and shape to put inside the heels and toes of the stockings. Then I will instruct thee on the weave stitch to use for the holes." Celia smiled and Elinore laughed again as she took the needle and yarn.

"I don't know how I would ever have endured these many many hours of waiting for suitors without you, Celia. It's hard enough not being able to ride my horse in the hills on these Test days. Without company I'd positively shrivel with boredom."

"Ah, my Elinore. I can think of no other mistress I would rather keep company with."

They worked in silence awhile. Several villagers on foot and in wagons passed by the royal stand taking goods between the village on the sea shore and the castle on the hill; all waved or called greetings to Elinore and Celia, who smiled in return. Celia started singing a lively folk tune, and Elinore joined in. As they finished, Elinore stood up and stretched, and her gaze drifted out to sea.

"I'm feeling restless today for some reason, Celia," she said after a pause. "Like a colt before a terrible storm. I feel an urge to run and run until the oppressive heaviness is left far behind."

Celia looked up at the absolutely clear sky, passed her arm across her forehead, then gazed silently at Elinore.

"Oh, it's nothing, Celia. I'll be all right." Elinore smiled. She turned away from the sea and picked another sock out of the basket. They worked again without speaking.

"I wonder how far he's gotten, Elinore," Celia finally broke the quiet. "I'm sure he's found the Golden Honeycomb in that awful beehive, and the Emerald Frog somewhere in those woods. And if he's any faster than that fellow last week, he will already have the Jade Statuette from Widow's Cave."

Elinore turned to Celia and laughed. "I still remember the time I got lost in there and you nearly worried yourself to death before Robert of Danforth found me. I think he was one of our stablehands then. That was the last time Father allowed me on the island until after I was thirteen, and then only with the closest of supervision." Elinore pulled another item of clothing from the basket as Celia stood to shake the thread scraps from her skirts.

"Do you think he's found the Diamond Fish yet, Elinore?"

Elinore looked up at the sun high in the sky. "If not, he should at least be searching the waterfall if he's going to find everything by sunset."

Celia shuddered. "And to think that poor Fritz fell all that way and we didn't even know till the next day."

Elinore still held her sewing unresumed in her lap. "And meanwhile we were searching the mainland woods and coastline, thinking he was trying to escape with some of the treasures like that horrid André." A tear glistened in the corner of her eye, but Elinore blinked it back. "I even liked him, Celia. In his perhaps less refined way, Fritz showed a kind heart. At least he was genuine. I just hope he didn't suffer much."

Celia put her mending back in the basket. "Come, my dear. Let's leave these sad thoughts and have some lunch. Then I think a little walk would do us some good."

Elinore's afternoon thoughts hovered around the Seven Treasures the suitor was to find. In addition to the four she had discussed with Celia that morning, he had to find the Pearl Berry in a patch of stinging nettle, the King's Seal (a duplicate of course) from a pool of pirana fish, and the Holy Scroll locked in a chest in a patch of quicksand. The suitor could use whatever means he desired to get to and from the island, but then must enter the depths of the island on foot, without weapons or tools, and use his wits and skills alone to obtain the Seven Treasures. Several suitors obtained serious injuries, and none escaped being a little worse the wear, including crushed pride, for their efforts. And to date, not a single man earned the coveted position of becoming husband to Princess Elinore and future heir to the throne.

"Father, are you sure you haven't made the Test too difficult?" Elinore had asked after several suitors had failed to obtain more than four or five objects, and one was fatally injured. "I know it's the traditional thing to do when one has no male heir, but I don't think it's right for people to suffer because of it."

"If they don't want to take the risks, they don't have to take the Test." the king replied mildly. "But you need not fear about finding someone who will pass it. He will come. Your great-grandfather passed this very test, you know."

"Yes, late 'in Spring when love in the air caused the trees to blossom', and the days were about an hour longer than they are now this late in the year." Elinore sighed. "I guess I just don't understand how it can be worth your time and their efforts to pass a test of physical endurance and searching skills. It seems to me a test of wisdom and political skills would be much more useful in determining a good ruler in this day and age."

"Elinore, this test is one of intelligence and perception as much as endurance, and therefore well qualified in its purpose. Your great-grandfather was a fine and wise ruler, and well respected by the people. The Test did its job well in selecting him. I'll hear no more about this now, child."

"I'm sorry father," said Elinore, going to him and giving him a kiss on the forehead. "I guess I'm just worrying more than I should without mother to talk to. I'm sure you know best."

King Louis watched his golden haired daughter leave his anteroom. She was blossoming in intelligence and independence as much as in beauty. He started talking as if in conversation with his departed wife. "Helenne, am I doing the right thing for our daughter? Surely the Test will determine which young man is most deserving of Elinore and the kingdom, won't it? I wish you were here now to give me your usual sound advice and encouragement!"

About an hour before dusk, King Louis returned to the stand where Elinore sat embroidering on a linen. Celia sat nearby with her mending, but no one else was in sight.

"It appears nothing is happening yet," he commented as he set down a basket whose contents were covered with a cheerful red cloth. "Monica sent us a picnic supper again." He sat down and stretched and sighed. "This is almost getting to be a pleasant habit, coming down to the seashore in the evening after court business all day."

Elinore nodded as she helped Celia pull out bread and cheese, chicken and fruit. As she ate, she looked out toward the island. How long would she have to wait before a suitor passed the Test? What kind of man would he be? She didn't really care what he looked like or what his origins were, as long as he was a kind and good man.

The sound of children's voices pulled her gaze to the beach in front of her. Five children were playing tag, laughing and calling excitedly. They were followed by two women, one cradling a newborn infant in her arms. A few minutes later an old couple, holding hands, joined them on the beach. All were there to watch the return of the suitor. Elinore felt an ache in her heart. What was it like to bear a child, the infant kicking inside her belly, or the baby nursing and looking up with trusting eyes, or the child laughing with joy while throwing its arms around her neck and calling her mama? And what heaven it must be to be joined in marriage with her best friend and to grow old together, savoring even the small moments spent in each other's company!

Elinore was jerked from her reverie by a shout from the small audience below. Her father beside her stood up and looked out to sea. The heads of a horse and rider were bobbing along the waves, growing steadily larger. Behind them the sky was turning golden and orange, and the sun drew relentlessly closer to the horizon. As he drew near, the rider began waving and shouting excitedly.

"Egad, he must have done it," muttered the king, looking surprised. Elinore stared at her father a moment, eyebrow raised, then turned back to get a closer look at this suitor, who was suddenly becoming a reality to her.

In a few minutes the horse stumbled onto the beach, and Prince Abram dismounted. His clothes were wet and somewhat tattered from the events of the day, but his bearing was proud and confident. He untied a bag at his waist and held it aloft. "Behold!" he cried to the audience on the beach. "The Seven Treasures of Rimrock Island! The Princess and the kingdom are mine!"

He turned toward the royal stand and approached it, followed by the small cheering crowd. The king was again seated. Prince Abram mounted the steps and, a smile playing on his lips, presented the bag containing the treasures to the king.

Elinore studied Prince Abram. His features were exotic, but handsome. His hair was dark and well groomed. His brown eyes were intense, but intelligent.

There was a tense silence while the king examined the seven objects. Then, raising his head, he smiled at Prince Abram and at his daughter. "Royal Subjects, Prince Abram has successfully completed the Test of Rimrock Island and found all seven treasures. He has now earned the right to my daughter's hand in marriage and to become heir to the throne."

The now growing crowd cheered. Elinore's gaze was again drawn to Prince Abram, standing before her. He was eyeing her from head to foot.

"You are truly as stunning as rumors stated," he said, nodding his head. He grasped her hand, drew it to his mouth, and kissed it. "My queen," he whispered, and his eyes glittered.

Elinore laughed nervously and withdrew her hand. "Prince Abram," she murmured.

The spectators erupted into another chorus of cheers. "Long live Princess Elinore! Long live Prince Abram!" A dry cloak was brought for Prince Abram to wear over his wet clothes. The royal carriage was brought up to the steps of the royal stand. Prince Abram took Elinore by the elbow and escorted her down the steps of the stand and into the carriage. Abram sat in the seat opposite Elinore and her father for the ride back to the castle, while a page followed with Abram's horse.

The long ride back up the mountain to the castle should have given Elinore plenty of opportunity to observe Abram, but every time she glanced in his direction, she found him staring directly at her with an intent piercing look in his eye that made her look away again.

"Abram, tell me a little about yourself," said King Louis after a period of silence.

"What would you like to know about me, Your Highness?" he responded, eyes still on Elinore.

"Tell me about your country, your family, your skills and interests."

"In my country, the customs are somewhat different from yours, as I have discovered. I have one older brother, who is heir to my father's property; the others are half brothers. My skills you observed today with the winning of the Test. As for my interests, at this moment I have only one."

Elinore didn't need to look at either one to know that both were staring at her. She kept her gaze fixed on the fields and trees moving past her carriage window, and spoke not a word.

Her father tried again. "Tell me, Abram, what would you do if political relations became strained between your country and ours?"

"I would do the only thing possible, act as intermediary until I had achieved again peaceful relations."

"And if that strategy didn't work?"

"If I desired it, it would," Abram said with finality.

Elinore's father pressed no further. They rode in complete silence the rest of the way back to the castle.

Supper was as strained as the carriage ride had been, with the king's questions and Prince Abram's brief answers being the sum of the conversation. For once Elinore found herself with nothing to say. When supper was finished and as soon as she politely could, she excused herself from the table. Abram immediately arose.

"May I speak with you, Princess?" he asked.

She nodded. "Go ahead, Prince Abram."

He looked around. "Not here. "The garden perhaps?"

Elinore glanced at her father. He nodded. "Yes, this way," she said. She led him out to the part of the garden near the fountains. The air was refreshing, and the moon was just coming up over the nearby trees.

"Princess," Abram began.

"You may call me Elinore," she interrupted quietly.

He went on. "You have said very little tonight, Princess. Did I offend you in some way?"

She smiled. "No. I just did not have much to say."

"I had understood that the women of your country are very forward. Is this not true?"

She looked surprised. "Forward? Not particularly." She paused. "Oh. If you mean we talk a lot or express our opinions, yes, you could call us forward. Especially compared to women of some other countries."

"Ah. That is what I thought." He took a few steps toward the fountain, and gazed at it in silence a moment, and clenched his fist. Suddenly, he turned toward Elinore, and grasping her face with his hands, leaned forward as if to kiss her. Startled, she let out a cry, wrenched herself free of his grasp, stepped back several feet, and stood looking at him, panting.

"Mister Abram," she finally gasped, poised and ready to run. "Whatever are you doing?"

A slow smile touched his face. "I was testing how forward the women of your country really are," he said.

"Not that forward," she said firmly. "I now bid you good night." She turned and walked quickly back into the castle, not once glancing behind.

In her room, dressed for bed and alone, Elinore found that her desire for sleep had left her. Thoughts whirled in her mind without direction.

"This should be the happiest day of my life," she told herself. "A suitor has finally passed the Test, yet I can't find it within myself to rejoice. I almost feel let down, disappointed. What kind of man was I looking for? Am I afraid of marriage, of a relationship with a man, of bearing children? I thought I was ready for these things, hungering for them. Am I afraid of walking that last step from childhood, and taking on the responsibilities of ruling a kingdom? What in the world is wrong with me?"

Elinore slipped out from under the covers of her bed, and made her way to her dressing table across the room. By the light of the moon entering the adjacent window, she poured herself a cup of water. She lifted the tumbler to her lips, froze in mid motion, then suddenly let it slip from her grasp to land clattering on the floor.

"I don't even know him," she thought, her fingers clutching the blouse of her nightgown. "I can't marry a man I don't know and love. He's a perfect stranger to my family, my country and its customs. How can I be sure he'll be a good husband and ruler even if he did pass the Test?" She stared out at the moon in silence a while longer. "I must do all I can to get to know him," she determined. "No judgements until all the information is in."

She suddenly realized she was shivering. She tried to locate the tumbler she had dropped, but was unable to find it in the dark. She dragged herself back to bed, where she eventually passed into fitful sleep.

CHAPTER 2

Touring the Kingdom

Elinore awoke to the clatter of horses' hooves in the courtyard below. She pulled a robe around her shoulders and went to the window. The light of dawn was just beginning to distinguish itself from night, yet already messengers were saddling up their mounts to herald around the land news of the winning of the Test and the forthcoming wedding feasts.

"I have only a few days to get to know this Prince Abram," she thought. "I must have him do things that will reveal to me his character. I hope for the sake of my people that he is a good and fair man, and for my sake that he . . ." Elinore shivered, but could not force her thoughts onward. She drew a deep breath. "It will be for him yet another test to win. May God be with me and with him."

She touched her forehead, heart, right and left shoulders, turned from the window, and knelt before her bed to start the day with prayer.

Elinore dressed in her most cheerful riding outfit and went downstairs for breakfast. Abram was in the great hall, examining the display of armory.

"That one belonged to my great great uncle, James the Fourteenth," Elinore spoke as she came up behind him. "He—"

Abram whirled, his hand on the hilt of his sword. On recognizing her, his hand dropped to his side, and he scanned the length of her with the corner of his mouth slightly upturned. "You are dazzling as the sun this morning, Princess. Do you always make such a contest with nature?"

In Abram's presence, Elinore suddenly didn't feel very dazzling at all. She donned her court smile and rallied the thoughts she had so carefully prepared moments earlier.

"Forgive me, Prince Abram, for my conduct last night. I fear my welcome fell a victim to my fatigue. But I should like to make amends and give you a tour of the kingdom today if you are agreeable."

"I should like that very much," He smiled and offered her his arm. "May we start with the work in this hall?"

She court-smiled again and put her fingers in the crook of his arm. She indicated the armor Abram had been studying. "Uncle James had no male heir, and neither did his brother, my great-great grandfather. My great grandfather passed the Test at Rimrock Island as you did, Prince Abram, and married into the family. He was too big a man to fit Uncle James' armor, and then his son wanted to

16

wear his father's. So this piece became a part of the armory museum."

After the armory, Elinore showed Prince Abram the portrait hall. "These are the portraits of my ancestors since the founding of our little nation of Sterling two hundred years ago. My grandfather had both a son and a daughter." She indicated the opposite wall. "My Aunt Lydia married King Charles of the neighboring kingdom of Adonia. We'll display the portrait of their son, Gilbert, when he becomes their king."

She looked up at Abram, who had been watching her intently as she spoke. Instinctively she started to look away, then caught herself and met his gaze. After a minute he was the one who broke the stare. "I believe it is time to go and partake of our morning repast, Prince Abram. Shall we?"

After breakfast Elinore led Abram to the stables. "I want you to meet Spirit." Abram raised his eyebrows. She explained. "My horse. I picked him out of the herd as a colt and trained him myself." She smiled. "He definitely fits his name. I am almost the only one who can ride him."

Abram looked aghast. "And your father lets you ride him?"

"Of course! Father feels that riding is one of the many skills a princess should know. Shall we go?"

Abram watched with lowered eyebrows as she saddled her horse and led him from the stable. Then he fetched his horse. It was apparent no one else was going with them. "I would not feel safe letting my queen out of the castle courtyard on horseback. And I would let her go nowhere without an escort of guards," he said.

She looked at him over her shoulder. "Would you prefer we bring an escort today?" She pulled a long dagger out of its sheath hidden in her skirts, handling it expertly. "Or do you think we just might be able to defend ourselves should something come up?"

He frowned briefly, then smiled. "Show me your kingdom." he said, and they left through the castle gates together.

They spent the morning touring the castle's neighboring lands. Near lunch time Elinore turned her horse toward the nearby town. "Let's get something to eat," she said.

Abram followed Elinore as she entered town, then turned onto a side street. He looked distinctly uncomfortable, and his hand holding the horse's reins were slower in giving their directions. She stopped in front of a building that said "Georgio's Inn" on a sign hanging overhead, and dismounted.

"Here we are," she said.

Abram frowned. "At a common eating place, Princess? Somehow this seems beneath your dignity."

"I know the owner, Mr. Abram. If you'd rather, I'll bring something out for you." She smiled coldly.

"I'll come," He dismounted. Grasping her elbow with one hand, and holding the other near his sword hilt, he pushed the door open with his shoulder and strode in, pulling her behind him. As the door flew open and they entered the eating hall, conversation fell silent. Abram paused, stared down the few who met his gaze, and led Elinore to one of the cleaner tables in a corner. Though customers started talking again, the volume remained much quieter than it had been before.

An aging woman came over. "What can I get you, dearie?" she grinned at Elinore and winked. Abram looked about to say something, then shut his mouth tightly.

"The usual, Petra," said the princess, smiling back. Elinore leaned toward Abram. "Do you trust me?" she asked. "The house special on Tuesdays is absolutely delicious. Petra makes it herself."

Abram eyed the woman's fading ribbons and slightly patched gown, then looked at Elinore. "As you wish, Princess. The house special."

When the steaming bowls arrived, Abram looked down at chunks of potato, vegetable and meat floating together in a sauce. "What in the world is this?" he asked, poking at a chunk of meat.

"Beef stew," Elinore answered, her mouth full. "And the funny thing about it, is that for almost every commoner this is a staple, while the castle folks have hardly even heard of it."

Abram took a small taste, then a larger one. Soon he too was cleaning the bowl. "I have never tasted anything like it," he said. "It is good."

Near the end of their meal, an older gentleman in worn vest and trousers came over. He took Elinore's hand and kissed it. "It is always a pleasure to have you come visit us, My Lady," he said in a rather gruff voice. "And I am always glad when you bring company." He bowed his head to Prince Abram.

"Master Georgio, this is His Highness, Prince Abram," Elinore said. "I am giving him a tour of our kingdom. It would not be complete without a taste of Madam Petra's cooking."

The innkeeper blushed. "You are too kind. My wife insists that this meal be on the house."

Abram smiled and nodded his head to accept the offer. "Oh, no!" Elinore cut in quickly. "I would not dream of it. I could not feel right coming again if I did not contribute my fair share." She pressed a coin into Georgio's hand. "If she does not agree, she must discuss it with me the next time I come."

As they left the inn, Abram helped Elinore onto her horse. "Are you sure it is proper and safe to associate with the common folk?" he asked.

She looked at him a long moment. "Is it that dangerous for women in the country you come from?" she asked. "Here the people watch out for each other. Of course there are highwaymen, but we also follow common sense and take guards when traveling beyond the village and castle lands. As for proper, is it not imperative for a sovereign to know how her people live?"

Abram did not answer. He mounted his horse and pulled it away from the inn with an impatient turn of his hand. "I am ready to return to the castle now, Princess."

Elinore was very glad to be back at the castle for a short rest in her room. It took a lot of effort to entertain Prince Abram. At least that is what it felt like, with the constant pressure to keep up conversation and hold her temper in. There had been many times through the course of the morning she had wanted to scream. What it was that bothered her she couldn't quite say; it was like having an itch she couldn't quite locate but that worsened the more she scratched around it. No, it was worse than that. She actually felt shivers when he stared at her. What did it take to connect with that man?

Elinore got off her bed and went out into the hall. Without at first realizing it, she found her feet taking her in the direction of the guest wing. As she walked, her thoughts turned inward pondering the mix of emotions she felt about this Abram, she heard two voices. Sometimes louder and sometimes softer, they were speaking in a fluid graceful language that she could not understand. She stopped to listen. There was a lull in the conversation, then she heard the louder imperious voice speaking in command tone, and then a smacking sound. There was silence, then a quick shuffling of feet, and a man emerged from a room down the hall, walking toward her, his head bowed slightly. He was dressed in the kind of clothes her people would wear, but he was bearded and his hair was dark like Prince Abram's. His right cheek appeared redder than the left, and a trickle of blood oozed from his right nostril. He did not wipe the blood away, nor did he look at her as he passed. Elinore stood against the wall, feeling like an intruder.

"Good afternoon, Princess," spoke Prince Abram's voice at her ear.

She jumped and whirled. She had not heard him approach. "Abram!" she said. She took a deep breath. "Are you ready for your afternoon tour?"

"What is the destination this time, Princess?"

"I thought I would show you Sterling's farms and lands, by coach." Elinore walked to the front entrance of the castle,

Abram keeping pace at her side. She had arranged for the coach driver and footman to meet her there. She would not be alone with Abram again.

Elinore kept the conversation on the geography of the land, the fishing ports, the history of their little country, the statistics of trade, productivity, and population growth. She was about to discuss some of the social problems they were struggling with, then hesitated.

"Prince Abram," she asked instead. "What are some of the social problems in your country? How do you deal with them?"

He looked genuinely perplexed. "Social problems? I do not understand. We have no social problems."

Elinore stared at him. Every country had social problems. "What do you do about those who steal? Who takes care of the orphans? How do you prevent unwed pregnancies? How do you take care of the poor?"

Abram looked at her and smiled. "We do not have problems with those things in my country. If a man were to steal, he would lose his hand; therefore no one steals. Adultery is punished by death by stoning; there are no unwed pregnancies. Families take care of their own; if a man were to die, his brother or father is duty bound to care for his children as his own. The loss of all four wives at once in a family is unheard of; there are no orphans. As for there being any poor, if a man is in debt and is unable to repay it, he sells off some of his servant's or his own children. If he is not able enough to make a living and care for his family, he is better off going into servitude himself and letting another care for them all."

Elinore leaned back in her seat and stared out the carriage window. Abram's solutions certainly were unique, some a little cruel. She could see how they might work, in the land where Abram was from. She was remembering some of the things her aged history professor had told her of some of his journeys in other lands. If she remembered correctly, Abram's country was more barren than her own, more desert-like. Perhaps harsh solutions were required in a harsh land. But would that be needed here? And would her people accept them? Doubtful.

She glanced at Abram. He was searching her again with his eyes and she looked away again, folding her arms across her waist. Would he be able to adjust to the customs of her country? Time would tell.

Elinore directed the coach driver to return to the castle. After dinner, King Louis took Abram and Elinore on a tour of the castle. Elinore was glad that her father mentioned nothing of secret passageways or surprise fortifications. However, Abram's eyes were sharp, and Elinore wondered how much he really discovered.

The King ended the tour at the guest hall. "We will let you retire now, Prince Abram," he said, smiling. "I would like to invite you to attend court with me on the morrow. I am interested in getting your viewpoint on the matters that arise in our kingdom. We begin right after breakfast."

Abram bowed his head. "I am honored, Your Highness."

King Louis left, and Elinore began to follow her father.

"May I bid you goodnight, Princess?" Abram asked.

She turned. "Good night, Prince Abram," she responded. "Pleasant dreams."

Abram reached for her hand, kissed it, and continued to hold it. "I dream of nothing but you, and it is always pleasant."

Elinore withdrew her hand and returned to her quarters. What was the matter with her? Prince Abram was all manners, and he seemed to be a romantic and attracted to her. So why wasn't she falling head over heels in love with him?

First of all, she was picturing marrying a man a little easier to talk to and with perhaps brown hair. Not that she was prejudiced; it would just take her a little more time to get used to him and see into his heart.

Secondly, his country's customs were in some ways quite different. She had a feeling he would continue to surprise her with his unusual approach to things. On the other hand, he might offer some wonderful solutions to some of her country's problems.

Her third concern was more instinctual. It bothered her when he stared at her. She should be flattered, but instead she felt . . . undressed. And what about his comment referring to families having four wives? He made it sound like a man would be married to all four at once. How odd! How frustrating! How immoral! Elinore sincerely hoped Abram planned to only be married to her. He better not already be married to someone else!

Elinore sat down on the edge of her bed, and sank her head into her hands. Her hands were trembling. What would happen if she refused to marry this Prince Abram? Her father would be disappointed in her, and his word, his royal promise would become untrustworthy before his people. And what would Prince Abram do? He might force Elinore to marry him anyway. She shuddered. Or he would return to his own country, and bring back an army to seek his revenge. It would be within his right. But her country was small, and though her people would fight well, the loss in a war would be severe. No, she could not do that to her people.

Elinore stood up and paced the floor. No, no matter what her own desires were, she must protect her people. It would be better for them if she relinquished her own dreams and married Prince Abram.

Now resolved to her mission, no matter how difficult it might be, she lay upon her bed. It was only after turning her thoughts to the pleasant days on the beach, sewing with Celia, and bantering with Robert of Danforth and others from the nearby village, that she was finally able to fall asleep.

CHAPTER 3

Caught in the Storm

In the morning Elinore awoke, washed and dabbed on her lilac-scented perfume. She dressed in her flowing gown of light spring blue, which particularly accented her rich golden hair. After tying her flowing hair back in a matching blue ribbon, she went down for breakfast.

Prince Abram was already seated with her father, waiting. Both stood when she entered. Prince Abram's eyebrows rose when he saw her, and a smile spread across his entire face. As Elinore allowed Abram to seat her, her father nodded approvingly.

Elinore started a more lively breakfast conversation, using topics and questions she had prepared that morning. Prince Abram mainly listened and watched while Elinore and her father did most of the talking. Then it was time to attend the court. Abram offered his arm which Elinore took, and they followed King Louis down the halls, into the courtroom, and up onto the royal dais. The king sat in the right hand chair, and indicated that Abram should take the one at his left. A servant brought a third chair, cushioned and soft, and placed it to the right of the king. Elinore sat in it, noting that it was more comfortable to her than the thrones originally made for the King and Queen. She made a mental note to herself to have at least one of the thrones refitted to fit her better. A little comfort here and there would be worth it after all, especially if she were going to spend long hours here. But not so comfortable that she could fall asleep while holding court!

Most of the morning passed with various people of the kingdom coming forth with questions or problems to ask the King. King Louis settled some of them quickly, and some of them with more thought. Several times the King leaned over to ask Prince Abram what he would do, sometimes using his ideas, sometimes not.

A couple of farmers came from a more distant village, concerned about some of their cattle dying. The local physician had given the sick animals some herbs, but the cattle were dying all the faster. Abram announced to the King that it was a cattle plague. Without dispute the affected cattle must all be destroyed by fire. All other animals and humans they had touched within the past month must be quarantined for a total of two months beyond any signs of further illness. The farms and the whole village must have no contact with other humans and animals during this period of time. The two traveling farmers must warn the people they had contacted in their journey here, and they must also observe this quarantine. Though the directions seemed severe, King Louis had no better idea to offer. He did, however, offer to compensate the villagers and farmers for their loss of animals. The two farmers left with grim expressions on their faces.

Another man came in dragging his teenage daughter behind him. She would slip out of the cottage at night to do who-knew-what, and sleep in late in the mornings, avoiding her share of the chores and field work. He had tried talking to her, forbidding her to visit friends, even beating her. Nothing seemed to be working. Elinore tried to talk with the girl, but she was sullen and silent. Abram advised the father to marry her off immediately to a man of his choice. The father's eyes lighted up, and pulled the daughter away, while she protested profusely.

Two more farmers came in, disputing ownership of a certain valuable milk cow. One man had originally bought her, then sold her to the other for a certain price. The price had not been paid in full, according to the one, and so the cow still belonged to him. The other vowed that he had paid to his very last farthing plus some produce from his fields, thus fulfilling the bargain. King Louis asked the first farmer what more was required to complete the sale. When the price was named, the second farmer looked crestfallen. It would be after next year's crops before he could pay that. Then what about selling the cow back to the original owner? But the money was spent, and the grass field to keep the cow had been planted in corn. Abram advised the King that the only solution was for the second farmer to sell one or more of his children to complete purchase of the cow, or to turn the cow over to the King to own. Both men looked horror stricken. Elinore then suggested that they share the use of the cow until one of the farmers could pay for it. Though the farmers looked uncomfortable at the thought of having to share, they agreed that this seemed the most fair.

Thus went the morning. Unique solutions were offered by Prince Abram. Some were excellent ideas, some very odd for the people to accept, some required Elinore's intervention to save the people from a fate worse than their original problem. As court ended for lunch, Prince Abram offered his arm again to Elinore to escort her out.

"Was I impressive, Princess?" he asked Elinore.

"Quite," she said coldly, and pretended not to see his extended arm. She walked quickly a few steps to catch up to her father, who was walking ahead of them. "Father," she said breathlessly. "I will not be attending court with you this afternoon. I have some urgent business to attend to."

King Louis stopped and looked into her eyes, searching them for a moment. "Is everything all right?" he asked softly. She nodded, not trusting her voice to speak. "Then go, daughter," he smiled, then turned and walked on.

Elinore paused and turned to Abram. "Excuse me, Prince Abram, I will join you again at supper time." Then she whirled quickly away from him, not looking back.

She took a side hallway to some stairs, and went down to the stables. Upon reaching them, she went to the stall housing Spirit. Burying her face in the warmth of his neck, she finally let flow the tears she had been holding back. Spirit turned and nuzzled her, whickering.

What was wrong with her? Despite her best intentions to give Abram a chance, to try and get to know him, she kept finding herself here, upset and running away! She must try to like this man for the sake of the kingdom!

Elinore suddenly realized that in her reverie she had bridled Spirit, swung onto his back and was riding out of the courtyard bareback. A ride through the meadows should heal her spirit. She kicked her heels into Spirit's sides and galloped away from the castle.

Her mind did clear somewhat from the exhilaration of the ride. As Spirit slowed to a lope and then a trot and walk, her thoughts returned to her problem. There had to be a way to solve this! Surely he could change his approach in the kingdom if properly taught. However, his demeanor this morning was proud, stubborn, all-knowing. He had not shown any inclination to listen to Elinore's ideas, and some of his most cruel ideas were only saved from implementation by the King's voice and decision. She could imagine Abram forbidding her to have a voice in the affairs of the kingdom, from visiting the village, from even riding her horse.

Anger boiled up inside her, and she kicked Spirit's sides again into a gallop. Forbid her from riding her horse and speaking her mind, hah! He might as well try to forbid a bird to fly! He could cage her up, but her soul would always be longing for the freedom of flight. And if he tried to impose his ideas and morals on her people, they would rebel too. No, much as she had tried to convince herself otherwise, this man would not be accepted as king over this little kingdom!

Elinore ran her horse over hills and valleys until his sides were lathered. As her anger abated, she let Spirit slow his pace, patting his sides as they both panted and caught their breaths. Looking up, she realized she had reached the foothills of the mountains, where the Dark Forest began. Thick rainclouds were rolling overhead, and as she turned her horse around, spatters of raindrops began to fall. She shivered as the wind whipped through her light dress despite the warmth of Spirit's hide beneath her. She better start homeward fast.

In a few minutes the rain was falling harder, and she was soon soaked to the skin. She led Spirit back toward the trees and searched for a rocky outcropping, a dry dense cluster of trees, anything to protect her from the storm.

Then she saw it, the opening to a shallow cave, just visible through a cluster of trees and dense foliage. She turned Spirit toward it. Suddenly, a man arose just in front of her, white teeth grinnning in a bearded face, the glint of a sword in his hand. Spirit reared. At her side Elinore felt as someone grasped the reins to Spirit's head, and she turned to stare into the face of a larger, brown haired fellow. His intent face looked strangely familiar, but Elinore felt frightened nonetheless. She snapped back on Spirit's reins, trying to pull him away from the bearded fellow, and Spirit reared again. This time his hoof struck the cheek of the dark haired man, knocking him to the ground. Kicking her foot against the still outstretched arm of the brown haired man, she finally managed to break Spirit free of his grasp. She clung to Spirit's back as he plunged through the trees, and out into open meadow. She did not slow him down as he streaked away from the hills.

Out in the fields the cold of the wind reached to her bones. There was no sign of the rain letting up, and her teeth were chattering uncontrollably. Oh, for a moment of warmth!

Then she saw a barn standing alone in a field off to her right. Feeling like a trespasser, though desperate, she trotted Spirit up to the large double door, then looked around. No one seemed to be here. She slid off her horse's back, lifted the latch to the barn door, and opened it. At one end were loose piles and bound bales of hay. At the other end, bags full of some kind of grain were piled high. The middle space was empty, but wheel tracks crossed over the floor as though a wagon were kept here.

Elinore led Spirit over to the loose piles of hay, and he began eating voraciously. She had not brought any coin with her, but she made a mental note to repay the landowner for whatever hay they used. Then she chose a clean pile of hay midway up the stack, nestled down, and pulled handfuls of hay over herself. It did not bring immediate heat, but her shivering stopped, and she began to feel a tiny bit warmer.

Suddenly the barn doors were thrown open, and a large man wrapped in furs led in a horse pulling a wagon. Never before had she been afraid for her safety among her people, but now she found her heart pounding, and vivid images and fearful possibilities ran through her mind. She shrank into her pile of straw, trying to stay unnoticed.

The man saw Spirit and stopped. He looked around the barn, and his eyes fell on Elinore.

"Hey, you there!" he said, coming toward her. "What are you doing in my barn?"

Elinore stood and glanced in the direction of her horse. There was no way she could make a run for Spirit, grazing as he was on the other side of the fur-covered man. She scrambled up from the straw, looking for another place she could run.

"Forgive me, kind sir," she panted. "I was caught in the storm. I did not know where else to turn. I will repay you for the straw my horse has eaten." The fur covered man was beginning to climb up the hill of straw. Elinore was shivering again, and her joints felt stiff from the cold. "Please don't hurt me," she squeaked.

The man in fur stopped and stared at her, then began to laugh. Then his laughter stopped. "Don't you know me, Princess?" he asked, beginning to unwrap his head furs.

Elinore's heart sank inside and she closed her eyes. It felt like a nightmare. Prince Abram called her "Princess" just like this.

"Nooo!" she almost panicked, then drew a deep breath and opened her eyes. The man had unwrapped his head furs, and it was not Prince Abram. She sank to her knees in the straw in relief. It was Robert of Danforth.

"Whoa! Easy there, my Lady!" cried Robert, leaping up the rest of the way to her side. "You look like you've been chased by gobblins! Not to mention being drowned in the rain. Here, put this on." He took off his fur coat and wrapped it around her shivering body. The warmth was heavenly.

She looked up at him gratefully. "Thank you, Robert of Danforth," she sighed.

He stepped back and looked at her. "I must admit, though, my Lady, that I did not recognize you at first, all bedraggled and covered with straw."

Elinore smiled at him. "I'm not exactly at my best today, am I, Robert? But I do apologize for entering onto your property. I didn't exactly come prepared for the wind and rain."

"Pshaw," Robert waved a hand. "I wasn't going to push you out, no matter who you were, as long as I knew your intent was not to attack me or steal from me. But enough of this. We must get you into something dry, and warming in front of a fire. Come get into my wagon and I'll take you to my cottage." He grinned. "It's not a palace, but it is nearby."

He helped her climb down from the straw pile and into his wagon. Spirit let Robert tie his reins to the wagon back. Then Robert pulled another fur from his wagon, threw it over his own shoulders, and jumped into the wagon seat beside her. He whacked the reins over his own horse and they were off, out into the storm again. Just around the bend in the road, Robert pulled up to the door of a neat little cottage with whitewashed walls. He helped her down from the wagon and let her in the front door.

"Make yourself comfortable," he said. "I'm taking the animals into the stable out of the rain."

Elinore sat down in the front room that doubled as living area and kitchen. Seeing a pile of wood against the wall, she pulled out some smaller sticks and began laying them inside the fireplace. Robert entered at that moment.

"Now, now, My Lady," he chided her. "You are a guest here. I'll take care of that." He added some dry leaves from a bin, and with a strike of his flint, started the flame. He took a cooking pot, filled it with water from a barrel by the door, and hung it on a hook over the fire. He then added a couple of small logs to the fire.

"I'm going to dry and rub down the animals, Princess," he said. "Your horse is staying calm next to my Bart. I will be right back."

Elinore leaned back in the chair and stretched her legs toward the warm flames. Yes, Spirit seemed to remember Robert from before, and was doing just fine. She closed her eyes.

The cottage door opened again. Robert took off his fur drape and hung it on a hook by the door. He washed his hands and face in a water basin there, and toweled dry. Then he took a ladle and tested the temperature of the water in the pot.

"Just a few more minutes and it will be hot enough for some tea, my Lady," he said. "But first we need to get you into some dry clothes." He looked down at the ground a moment. "I am afraid, my Lady, that I only have my clothes to offer you. I hope that you will not be offended."

Elinore laughed. "Robert, you have been very generous. I think I can stand to wear your clothes for a while. It has got to be more comfortable than my soaked linens."

"Very well, then." Robert went through a door at the back of the room. Elinore could hear various noises, a trunk being opened, the rustling of things being pushed here and there. Then he returned. "I have laid out some garments that should be suitable. You may change in the back chamber."

Elinore went back through the door. It was a small room, packed on shelves and hooks with various items used for living. On the narrow bed were laid a pair of leather knicker pants, a long sleeved shirt, vest and stockings. Though not new appearing, they were in good repair, and they smelled clean. Elinore peeled off her wet dress and undergarments, and pulled on the dry clothes. Though big, the pants had a drawstring at the waist she could tighten. The shirt also was loose, but manageable when she rolled up the sleeves and tied the laces at the chest. The vest added a little modesty. She rolled her wet things together and returned before the fire. Robert was pouring cups of tea. He stopped and looked at her.

"Not as elegant as your blue dress, I'm afraid," he said. "But you still look lovely."

"With my matted, tangled hair," she began. "I could be called anything but that."

He snapped his fingers. "Yes!" he said. He dashed into the back room and reappeared with a carved bone comb. He washed it in the water basin, then handed it to her. "You are welcome to us this, my Lady, if you desire."

Elinore sipped on her tea while she combed the tangles out of her hair. Robert sat in his chair, cutting vegetables for a soup and intermittently watching her.

"You haven't told me yet how you ended up caught in a storm way out here by the Dark Forest," Robert commented quietly.

Elinore stopped the combing and looked down at her hands holding the comb in her lap. "I was out riding to think things out, and lost track of where I was," she said. She remained fiddling with the comb in her lap.

"It's a big change, getting married," he said, voice still soft. "The news has already traveled to neighboring towns. I heard on my trading trip."

She looked up at him, and their eyes met. Suddenly she was on her knees before him, the tears flowing down her cheeks.

"I don't know who to talk to, Robert," she confessed. "Prince Abram passed the Test, and I'm supposed to marry him, but something about him makes me uncomfortable." She drew a deep breath. "That I can bear, except I'm concerned whether he is good for my people. He has such . . . such strange ideas sometimes." She gulped some tears. "And then something else bothers me. His manservant, Rala, . . . well, I ran into him at a cave at the edge of the Dark Forest with someone else I thought I knew . . ." Her eyes widened. "It was that André fellow, who tried to pass the Test a couple of months ago, and attempted to steal a couple of the . . ." She stopped and shivered. "Something does not feel right about this whole thing, and I can't figure out what they are doing together."

She put her hand to her forehead. "I should not have told you all of this." She looked Robert in the eyes. "I feel like I can talk to you as a friend, but I suppose all that will have to change when I am married."

Robert had stopped his vegetable paring to listen, and now he grasped her hands. His eyes shone. "My Lady," he vowed. "I will do all in my power to help you. You have my word."

Elinore nodded and wiped her tears. Then she watched as he poured the vegetables into the pot.

"Another cup of tea, Princess?" Robert asked.

"Yes, thank you." She sighed and settled back into her seat. There was silence for awhile as they sipped their tea again. "Robert," she suddenly asked. "What brought you here all the way from Danforth? Originally?"

"Well, I was a third son, and my two older brothers inherited all of my father's business. So I was appreciced out to your livery master here. I had always wanted to be master of my own lands, so I saved what I could, and when my apprentiship was over, I chose a horse as final pay and bought this land. I did have to clear a lot of it before I could plant, but it is my own. And this house I built myself." He looked around proudly.

"But you are not yet married?" Elinore queried.

Robert chuckled. "I had not found the right lady yet," he said, and his gaze held hers steadily.

Elinore dropped her eyes first. "I should be getting back home," she said.

"It's still pouring out there," said Robert drily. "At least eat something before you go."

Elinore's stomach growled and she smiled sheepishly. "I am hungry," she said. "I guess I forgot to eat any lunch."

As they finished their supper, the rain turned to a slow drizzle and then stopped.

"This is my cue," sighed Elinore. "I truly thank you, Robert, for your hospitality." She examined her bundle of wet clothes. "I wonder. Do you mind loaning me this outfit to get home in?"

"By all means, My Lady," he smiled. "in fact, I have a cloak for you too." He went out to the stable for a moment, and returned with a bundle of furs. Unwrapping the outer dark one, he pulled out a bluish white hunting cap. "For your father, His Majesty," said Robert, placing it gently on her head. He hesitated slightly, then reached into the bundle. He pulled out a full length cape of pure white fur. "I thought of you, my Lady, when I found this. I . . . I didn't know if I would actually ever give it to you, but fate brought you here in need of it. Take it. It is a gift."

Elinore drew it around her shoulders and fastened it at the neck. The inner lining was a light pink silk. "Oh, it is lovely," she breathed. She looked up at Robert's beaming face. She knew it must have cost him a fortune. She would have to find something worthy to give in return. "My many thanks," she said, and kissed him lightly on the cheek.

While she pulled her dress shoes on over the thick wool socks, Robert brought Spirit around to the door. He helped her on, pointed her in the direction she should go, and with a wave she was gone.

On reaching the castle, Elinore brushed down Spirit, amidst stares from the stablehands. Then with her bundle of wet clothes in one arm, and the fur cape draped over the other, she ran up the stable steps into the castle hall.

There she came face to face with Prince Abram. He eyed her strange attire with dark lowered brows. "What have you been up to this afternoon, Princess?"

She shrugged. "Getting caught in a thunderstorm," she said, trying to walk by.

He fingered the coarse fabric of her shirt sleeve, and then the softness of the white fur cloak. "Interesting attire for a lady who slipped out in a mere blue dress."

She blushed slightly. "A peasant took pity on me and loaned me some dry things."

"Including the cloak, Princess?"

"A gift from a friend."

As she pushed past him, she heard his parting comment. "Chastity and fidelity become all women, including royalty."

Blushing hotly, she fled to her room. How dare he assume something had happened—. Then she stopped short. Something had happened back there in Robert of Danforth's cottage. Not what Abram had intimated, but something almost as serious. She had opened her heart to another man! She had not imagined before that the situation could get any worse, and now—! She reached her room and threw herself on the bed, sobbing.

A servant called her to supper, but she sent the message that she had already eaten. Then she washed her face, sat in front of her mirror, and stared at her reflection. After an hour, she could see no other alternative. She resolved once again to go through with the marriage with Abram, to do her best to protect her people.

She changed out of the borrowed shirt and trousers, folding them carefully together. Then she put on another simple dress and went downstairs. Apparently Prince Abram had retired to his quarters, so Elinore joined her father in the library. He was reviewing some of the texts again about the procedures for adopting a new Prince into the line of heirs. When he saw Elinore, King Louis closed his books carefully and came over to sit next to her. She said nothing, so he grasped her hand and held it awhile.

"Tomorrow the dressmakers want to work with you on measurements and fitting for your wedding dress. Have you decided on the style you want?"

Elinore shook her head. Oh, she had looked at the various sketches of ideas, but before now getting married had seemed so far away she had not chosen a dress. Now the day was quickly arriving, but her heart was not in it. Any dress would do. She sat up a little straighter. No, this was her only wedding day. She would choose something stunning and enjoy the moment.

She smiled up at her father. "I do have some ideas though, Daddy." She giggled at her childhood name of endearment slipping out. "I want 'V' shaped necklines and waist in front and back of the bodice. The sleeves will be big puffs of satin at the shoulders, narrowing to a "V" point over the hand. Then it will have a full satin skirt with a train as long as I am tall, maybe with bows at the hem and at the back of the waist "V". I'd like to wear Mother's diamond bracelet, necklace and earrings." She furrowed her brows. "I can't decide on a tall point hat draping the veil, or a diamond tiara crown."

King Louis laughed. "If you choose the crown, I'll have to get the jewelers working on it at once, or we'll have to postpone the wedding."

"What about your grandmother's crown?" suggested Elinore. "She had it made with white gold, which would be perfect with my white dress!"

"Yes, that would work. It sounds to me as though you have your dress planned out after all, my daughter," he smiled.

She laughed. "I guess I do, Daddy." She kissed him on the cheek. "And what about the festivities?"

The King stroked his chin with his thumb. "We invite the Lords and Dukes and neighboring Kings, of course, to the wedding ceremony. I thought we would open the castle courtyard to the people of our land to come celebrate. We would serve a variety of feast delectibles. We would have entertainment, jugglers and acrobats, street actors and musicians. Have I left anything out, my dear?"

Elinore thought. "Would the courtyard be large enough for the crowds? I think we should hold it in the fields surrounding the castle."

The King nodded. "Yes, that would be better. What music would you like for the promenade entrance and exit?"

"I'll have to think on that one, Father."

King Louis gazed at Elinore. "Are you ready to be a wife, my daughter?"

Elinore's expression froze. Slowly she brought her hands together in her lap and bowed her head slightly, her voice subdued. "Yes, Father. I suppose I am ready."

The King gazed at her a little longer. "You look tired, my child. Why don't you go to bed now? Tomorrow is another long day." He stood, raised Elinore to her feet, then embraced her. "I love you, Elinore. I am proud of you, daughter."

CHAPTER 4

The Second Suitor

The next day Elinore was awakened early by Celia. "Eat a quick breakfast, my Lady. The dressmakers are waiting."

Elinore spent her morning and afternoon mostly standing while dressmakers measured and held fabric up to her. The master dressmaker gave directions constantly, striving and sweating to make sure the gown turned out as Elinore had described it to him. Ladies and men cut and sewed carefully but furiously, one here pouffing a sleeve, another there making bows, and another fastening seams. By late afternoon the dress was taking form, and Elinore was allowed to leave and prepare to eat dinner with her father and Prince Abram.

After dinner, Prince Abram excused himself, saying he had some business to attend to. King Louis retired to the library, and Elinore wandered the castle halls. Castle workers by now had returned to their homes, and she found herself back in the library, where her father was once again intently searching old books. Elinore stretched out on a long chair in front of the fire, and watched him.

"Are you looking for more ways to adopt a Prince?" she asked drily.

The King looked up and stared at her for a minute. "Actually I'm not," he said. "I'm looking up something else entirely."

"Some new problem with the subjects?" she asked. "If you tell me what it is, maybe I can help you."

"No, it is not. Well, not exactly, Elinore." He sat back in his chair and searched her face again. "I wasn't going to tell you until I found an answer, but I'm inclined to make a decision myself if I don't find any rule or law soon. It involves you, Elinore."

She sat up at the seriousness in his voice. What was he talking about? Did it have to do with her being seen in men's clothes the day before?

"Elinore," King Louis paused. "A young man approached me today. He petitioned me to grant him an opportunity to take the Test, as a suitor seeking your hand in marriage."

"What?" Elinore was startled. "Was he not aware that a suitor has already passed the Test and won my hand in marriage? I cannot marry two men."

"He was very aware of that fact." The King sighed. "He has challenged Prince Abram's right to marry you. He states he is ready to take the Test at Rimrock Island, and perform any other task I choose to set before him. He begged only that I not deny him the opportunity to try." King Louis looked over his spectacles at his daughter. "And he asks that I not reveal his name until I agree to the contest."

Elinore sat stunned. Who could this suitor possibly be? Was this legal, to allow him to try? Elinore's heart felt a leap of hope she had thought never to feel again. "Is there a precedent for such a thing?" she asked, barely daring to take a breath.

"That, my daughter, is exactly what I am searching for." He reached for his books again. Elinore picked up a book and began reading through it herself. This one seemed to be full of laws for handling things like what to do when a peasant tramples his neighbor's beans and such. She closed the book again and laid her chin in her hand.

"Father, where's the book telling about Great-grandfather's passing of the Test? That should contain a specific answer in it."

"I don't recall reading anything like this," commented King Louis, stroking his chin again. "But you are certainly welcome to look through it again." He indicated a newer appearing book already laid on his desk.

Elinore picked it up and skimmed through it. It described the situation of lack of male heirs, requiring the creation of a test to determine an appropriate consort for the daughter in line for the throne. It listed the rules for the Test, the ceremony for inducting the new Prince into his position, what powers and limitations might be placed on him. It recorded in detail what had actually happened with every suitor's attempt, and her Great-grandfather in particular. Various other rules were listed in the back index, many of which had no bearing on the Test-taking that Elinore could tell. She put the book down.

"You're right, Father. There is nothing helpful there."

"I do hope we find something," her father commented. "I dislike making new rules when it comes to something as important as marriage."

Elinore looked at him in surprise. "I didn't know you had such a vested interest in my marriage," she said.

He smiled at her. "You're my only daughter. I want your marriage to be to the right person."

Elinore gave him a hug, then looked at the books and thought again. "Has anyone in any other kingdom written rules on a similar situation?"

The King snapped his fingers. "That's it, my daughter!" Then his eyebrows drew together. "But who?"

"Oh, if I could only remember my history a little better," moaned Elinore. "There was someone a couple of hundred years ago, but who was it? I think it was in one of the countries on the plains."

"Yes! I believe it was near Egelshire. Let's see. It should be in one of these books." King Louis pulled down three volumes from his shelves and handed one to Elinore. They pored over them for another hour.

At last Elinore leaned back in her chair and closed her book. "I can barely focus my eyes any longer," she sighed. "I'll have to continue in the morning."

"That's fine, my daughter," said King Louis, looking up. "I think I'll continue a little longer here. I promised that young man an answer sometime tomorrow. Goodnight, Elinore."

"Goodnight, Father," she said, kissing him on the cheek. "I'll see you in the morning."

Both Elinore and her father slept through breakfast time the next morning. As the King rushed off to hold court, a servant handed him a piece of bread and cheese. Elinore wandered into the kitchen, found chunks of bread and cheese herself, and sat on a stool watching the cooks hurry around, mixing and baking. Her Aunt Lydia would be arriving at noon from the neighboring kingdom of Adonia, where she was married to the king.

Elinore and Prince Abram were just sitting down to midday dinner, when her father and Aunt Lydia came in.

"Oh, that's easy," Aunt Lydia was saying. "It's found in the National Book of Rules of Etiquette. I'll look it up for you after din—" She saw Prince Abram and stopped mid phrase. "You must be the young man who passed the Test. I am Lydia, Queen of Adonia, but that doesn't matter. I'm Elinore's aunt, King Louis' sister."

"Enchanted, Madam," Prince Abram stood, took Queen Lydia's hand, and bowed over it with a flourish.

"Oh, my darling niece," Lydia embraced Elinore warmly, then stepped back slightly. "Let me look at you. Oh my, you are indeed a grown up, lovely young woman."

Elinore lowered her head and smiled. "Oh, Aunt Lydia." Then she looked up at her again. "I am indeed glad you are here," and Elinore gave her another hug.

After dinner Lydia and King Louis went to the library before attending court again. Elinore was requested by the dressmakers to try on her wedding gown again. After a couple of hours they let her go. Outside the door she met Prince Abram. He was pacing.

"What is the meaning of this?" he asked, his face angry.

"I-I'm just trying on the wedding dress," Elinore's voice faltered.

He shook his head forcefully. "Come." He took her elbow, a little roughly, and walked her quickly down the hall. As they turned a corner, they met a couple of servants standing.

". . . another suitor to take the Test," one was saying in a loud whisper. The other servant nudged him, and they both looked up at Elinore and Abram. With wide eyes and red faces they scattered in different directions, the one passing them bowing his head briefly in obeisance.

Abram turned Elinore to face him. "All over the castle," Abram stated harshly. "Dread rumors are flying. Another suitor taking the Test? *I* passed the Test!! Your father cannot do this to me."

"Come," said Elinore firmly. "Let's go talk to Father."

Several folk from the kingdom were waiting in the courtroom to talk to the King. The King was listening to an old man, holding his hat in his hand, earnestly explaining his problem. Prince Abram walked in past the waiting peasants, and up past the old man. Elinore followed him a couple of steps behind.

"Your Majesty," Abram interrupted. "What is the meaning in allowing another suitor to take the Test that I passed?" All talking in the hall ceased, and everyone looked on in total silence.

King Louis cleared his throat. "Another suitor appeared requesting earnestly to take the Test."

"And you agreed to this?" Abram kept his voice in tight control, but Elinore could hear the strain. "What, am I not good enough for your daughter?"

Lydia, sitting next to the King, leaned forward, holding a book in her hand. A ribbon marked a page in it, and she opened to it. "You will find, Prince Abram, that rules for this sort of thing have been well established. It says here that a period of a fortnight is allowed for any challengers to the winner of a test such as this to come forward. This man appeared in three days. The King is obligated to agree to the challenge."

Abram looked at the words in the book, then stared from Lydia to King Louis, who nodded in agreement to her words.

"Very well, then," said Abram, voice still even. "We will see if he can accomplish the feat. If he does, then I have a right to challenge him myself."

"That is fair," agreed the King. "The test at Rimrock Island is being prepared even now as we speak, and will be held on the morrow."

Prince Abram turned on his heel and left the silent courtroom. Elinore smiled wonderlingly at her father and aunt, and followed Abram out.

The next morning before dawn, King Louis and Queen Lydia, Elinore and Prince Abram settled into the reviewing stand that had been re-erected on the shore in front of Rimrock Island. Shortly thereafter a man riding a horse appeared, stopped in front of the stand, and dismounted. As he climbed up the steps Elinore gasped. The man glanced at her briefly, then bowed before the King.

"Your Majesty," he said. "I am ready to take the Test."

"You understand the task and the rules?" asked the King. The young man nodded soberly. "Then, Robert of Danforth, prepare to start the Test."

Robert nodded and stood. He bowed to Lydia, then stopped in front of Elinore. Their eyes locked. Elinore said nothing, but her eyes shone. She offered her hand and he kissed it gently. Then Robert's eyes moved to Prince Abram's. They stared at each other for several long minutes, neither willing to break the gaze.

The King cleared his throat. "The dawn begins."

After another moment of visual dueling, Robert turned away. He ran down the steps of the stand, glanced at the sky's brightening colors, and leaped on his faithful horse, Bart. The sun's edge peeked over the horizon.

"Now!" cried the King. Robert dug his heels into his horse's side, which leaped down the beach and into the waves. Elinore watched intently until his form reached the island and disappeared. Then she sat back in her seat with a barely audible sigh.

Abram was searching her with his eyes. "He is the one, isn't he, Princess?"

"The one what?" she asked, innocently.

"The one you spent the afternoon with after the thunderstorm," he smiled coldly. "The one who has claimed your heart."

King Louis and Queen Lydia were watching her too. Elinore said nothing, just turned and watched the island again.

Abram leaned over to whisper in her ear. "I'm not blind, Princess. You shall see who is the most worthy."

The day was long. None of the four royal watchers left the beach area. Lydia and Louis were chatting about various issues they had to deal with in their kingdoms. Elinore longed for Celia's easy chatter. Instead she had Prince Abram's heavy presence, with his short answers and long silences.

Mid morning as it grew hotter, Elinore couldn't stand it any longer. She pulled off her shoes and stockings, gathered her skirts in her hands, and with a backwards glance at Abram, and a beckon of her head, she hopped down the steps of the reviewing stand and down to the beach. Abram caught up to her as she reached the water. Laughing and skipping in the waves, she felt cool and free at last. Abram watched her soberly, then sat down to pull off his shoes and socks too. Elinore stopped to watch him. He pulled his leggings up to his knees, then walked down to the water's edge. As the first wave washed sand up and back over his bare feet, his eyes widened in surprise.

"This is a very appealing sensation, Princess," he confessed. "We do not have any beaches such as this in my country. Merely a few streams, and many rock and sand hills."

After wave running awhile, Elinore threw herself down on the beach sand, gazing up into the sky. She felt Abram lie down beside her. Rolling over onto her stomach, then scooting onto her knees, she began digging a hole in the damp sand. Abram watched her curiously. After a few minutes, she began molding walls and towers around the hole. Suddenly understanding, Abram joined in to the digging and shaping. As they were completing the sand castle, a voice called them to lunch.

Elinore showed Abram how to wash the sand off their legs and hands in the waves, then they returned to the stand to eat. Celia was there with a basket of food.

"Ah, my mistress," said Celia, winking at her. "You have a healthy glow to your cheeks." She looked at Prince Abram. "As do you, my lord."

Elinore grinned. "And a healthy appetite to go with it," she commented, looking through the basket and handing out fruit, bread and cheese to everyone.

King Louis shook his head. "Do you see what I have to put up with?" he confided to Lydia, smiling. "I try to make a proper lady out of her, then she comes down to the beach and does this. Do you see why I despaired of ever marrying her off?"

"That doesn't seem to be your problem now, dear brother," returned Lydia wryly. "She may have two suitors to choose from at the end of the day."

After lunch Elinore felt ready for a rest. With Aunt Lydia and King Louis taking a walk down the beach, though, Elinore was a little leery of lying down again. Celia picked up the picnic basket as if to go.

"Oh, Celia, don't go," begged Elinore. She sat down on the floor of the stand and draped herself across one of the seats. "Stay and tell us one of your grand saga stories. I don't think Prince Abram is familiar with our legends."

Abram shook his head, and Celia smiled, settling herself on one of the seats. "Which one shall I tell, now? I know. I'll tell the one about how our country got started."

Abram chose a seat next to Elinore, and Celia put her hands on her knees and started. As Celia's sing-song voice went on, Elinore's eyes closed. She began thinking again about Robert of Danforth, on Rimrock Island hunting for the Seven Treasures of the Test. She prayed in her heart he would be successful. Then she fell asleep.

She awoke when the late afternoon sun hung over the hills in the west. She was no longer draped over the seat of her chair, but lying with her head on someone's lap. She quietly turned her head upward. It was Prince Abram's. He had sat himself down next to her, his back against the inside wall of the wooden stand, moved her to a more shaded and comfortable position, and fallen asleep himself. Celia was sleeping on the floor beside them.

Elinore sat up quickly. Prince Abram opened his eyes, stretched his arms and jiggled his legs. Celia rolled over and sat up, rubbing her eyes.

"I didn't finish the saga yet," Celia mumbled sleepily.

"That's all right," said Elinore. "I missed a lot of it anyway." Elinore looked around for her father and Aunt Lydia. They were sitting on the steps of the reviewing stand, which was now in shadows, chatting quietly.

"He comes," Celia announced.

At first Elinore wasn't sure what Celia meant. Then, looking toward the island, she saw a small figure on a horse splashing from the shore into the waves. It was Robert, returning. Everyone quickly took their places. The King checked the position of the sun. There was perhaps half an hour left till the sun would be low enough to set. Had Robert of Danforth found all seven treasures?

Robert arrived much as the other suitors had, tired, scratched up a little, and wet. But a smile played at the corners of his lips. He galloped up to the reviewing stand, jumped off his horse and dropped the reins. As he mounted the steps he glanced once at Elinore. She drew in an inadvertant breath. Robert knelt before the king and presented his bag of treasures.

"I have found the Seven Treasures, Your Highness," he announced.

Beside her, Elinore felt Abram stiffen. All watched closely as King Louis examined the Seven Treasures carefully. Finally he raised his head.

"They are all here. Elinore," he said, turning to her. "You now have two suitors who have claim to the kingdom and your hand in marriage. But you can only choose one."

Prince Abram stood. "I was the first. I claim the right to challenge this newcomer in a dual of strength and skill."

Princess Elinore stood and stared Prince Abram in the eye. "I too claim the right to propose a challenge. It will be a test of wit and worthiness."

The King interrupted their staredown. "So be it," he announced. "We return to the castle for dinner, and to prepare for Prince Abram's contest on the morrow."

In the carriage, Prince Abram made a point of taking the seat next to Elinore. Robert took the seat across from her next to the King. As the carriage bagan to move, Robert glanced cautiously at Elinore. She smiled at him, warmly and heartfelt. Robert then gazed at Abram intently, evaluating. Abram stared back at Robert, guarded, calculating. Robert smiled slightly. Abram put his arm around Elinore's shoulders, eyebrows lowering slightly. Robert raised his right eyebrow. Abram raised his chin.

Elinore looked at her father, and his expression was guarded. She nodded slightly, and looked out the window. One part of her was hopeful and delighted at Robert's passing the Test. Here was a chance to marry someone she knew something about and even liked! But there was a weight in the pit of her stomach. Things now were deadly serious, and there was no guarantee Robert would pass the remaining challenges. She prayed he would at least survive Abram's test.

Elinore thought again about the challenge she had proposed, a "test of wit and worthiness". She had to devise a test that was fair, but telling, that only the best suitor could win. It must prove his interest in and understanding of the people he must rule, and the honesty of his intent in seeking the position of king. It must show that the suitor's interest and love for her was true, above the riches of the kingdom or the power of the position as ruler. But the details of how to devise such a test eluded her. Perhaps Aunt Lydia would have some ideas.

At dinner that evening, the silent visual jousting between Abram and Robert continued. Then the suitors visited in private with the King, discussing Abram's test. Afterward Abram retired to his quarters in the East guest wing, while Robert was shown his room in the slightly older West wing. Elinore visited her Aunt Lydia in her suites to talk.

On hearing Elinore's criteria for her test, Aunt Lydia thought for several minutes. "I think, Elinore, my dear," she said at last. "We need to set up a political situation that has an easy but dishonest solution, versus a difficult but honest solution." She sighed. "When did you say you needed this ready by?"

"The day after tomorrow at the earliest, perhaps the day after, depending on the length of Abram's test," answered Elinore.

Lydia shook her head. "I might not be able to prepare quite that quickly, even under the best circumstances. Three days is what I require. Elinore, I need you to start another task for the suitors, preferably one that will take two to three days, that will appear to be the main test. The success of my plan depends on them not knowing when the real test is occuring."

"What are you going to do, Aunt Lydia?" Elinore asked.

Queen Lydia laid a finger across her own lips. "Ah, I cannot tell you. You too must not know the details, for the suitors to be convinced. You shall see as it unfolds."

"Thank you, Aunt Lydia," Elinore hugged her tightly.

"Now go to bed, child. There will be much to do this week." Lydia escorted her to the door, kissed her on the cheek, and closed her door.

CHAPTER 5

The Test of Strength and Skill

Elinore slept well despite falling asleep trying to come up with a task for the suitors. In the morning she discovered that Aunt Lydia was gone, having left early on some "urgent business". Elinore ate breakfast with her father, while each suitor fasted alone in his chambers. At the beginning of the ninth hour, Elinore and King Louis entered a balcony overlooking an enclosed courtyard. The suitors entered from either side.

Prince Abram was dressed in colorful robes, several layers thick, that covered him from wrist to ankle. His feet were shod with leather boots that gathered his pants in below the knee. A thick sash was tied around the waist, gathering in the tunic of thick, red fabric covering his torso. Around his head was wrapped a thick turban, with a cloth hanging from it around his neck and shoulders. At his left hip hung a curved scabbard, but it was empty.

Robert of Danforth on the other side of the courtyard was dressed in thick layers of leather, that like Abram, covered him from wrist to ankle. He too wore leather boots up to his knees, and a leather tunic belted in at the waist. On his head he wore a thick leather helmet, with flaps covering his ears and neck. Leather gloves covered his hands. He too had no weapon.

At a signal from the King, several servants came forward with a variety of weapons, swords, maces, spears. Abram chose a curved cimeter that matched the design work of his scabbard. Robert chose a medium sized, single bladed battle axe.

Elinore now noticed a structure in the middle of the courtyard. Two wooden scaffolds about twenty feet high supported between them a single log about one foot in diameter. Each suitor climbed a scaffold and stood at the top, eying the other.

King Louis spoke. "Each of you contestants understands the rules?" He asked. Both of them nodded. "Good. Remember the object is not to slay the other, but only to knock your opponent off the log. If sun sets before anyone falls, then it is a draw. Are you ready?"

Again they nodded, their bodies poised and ready.

"Begin!"

Both of the men began to move forward, feeling his footing on the straight log, neither taking his eyes off the other. Then suddenly Abram was leaping forward, sword flashing in the sunlight. Robert held his ground, blocking

Abram's sword thrusts with the shaft of his axe. Then the axe was swinging toward Abram, and he leapt back, deftly keeping his balance. Robert followed, Abram now using his sword to block the blows. Back and forth they went, swinging, parrying, thrusting. Elinore now observed that what had appeared to be sturdy leather boots on both their feet were actually leather feet protectors with flexible soles for easier gripping.

For an hour the men parried, neither able to knock his opponent off the log. Their thick clothing protected them from any serious injury, but slash marks and tatters were abundant.

Suddenly Abram lunged, driving his cimeter straight at Robert's face. Robert ducked, nearly losing his balance, then grasped the log beneath him and rolled into Abram's knees. Abram now was caught off balance, falling forward and to the side. With a terrific twisting of his body, Abram managed to grasp the log with one hand and one arm, but the momentum knocked the cimeter from his hand. As Robert regained his foothold and turned around, Abram hefted himself back onto the log. Robert heard Abram's cimeter clatter to the stones below, and noticed that his opponent stood unarmed. He stood for a moment, battle axe in hand, then tossed it too to the ground below. As it landed with a clang, Abram grinned.

Now the contest became a boxing and wrestling match. Again neither could quite get the upperhand on the other. Another hour passed as the sun grew hotter and their sweat poured down. Then Robert got hold of Abram's middle in a grip that took his breath away.

Suddenly Abram moved and twisted, sunlight flashing off something in his hand. Elinore screamed as Abram brought his hand down hard on Robert's back. Robert's grip around Abram loosened, and he toppled backward over the side of the log. As he fell, his flailing hand caught hold of Abram's ankle, jerking it out from under him. Both men sailed off the log toward the cobblestone ground below. Robert landed full on his back, Abram on his feet and hands beside him. Elinore watched, horrified, as Robert didn't move. Abram stood up, and walked over to pick up his sword. Elinore left the balcony and raced down the stairs to the courtyard below.

When she reached Robert, he still wasn't moving. She knelt over him and glared up at Abram. "What did you do to him, Abram?" she demanded. "I saw you hit him with something!"

Abram laughed harshly and showed her his open hands. "I have no weapons. As is the rule."

Elinore saw the sun glint off something again on his left hand. She leapt up and grasped his hand to look. A thick banded gold ring encircled his middle finger, supporting a large diamond.

"You hit him with this," she accused him.

Abram shook his head. "I hit him with the edge of my hand," Abram explained, demonstrating for her a chopping motion downward. "Use this across the back with enough force, and it works every time."

Robert groaned, and Elinore knelt again by his side. "Robert, Robert. Are you all right?"

His eyes fluttered partially open, and he gazed at her face. "Princess," he murmured, smiling. Then he opened his eyes wide and stared at Abram. He pushed Elinore away and struggled to sit up. "I've got to get back on my feet."

"No, Robert," said Elinore, pushing him back down. "The contest is over. Just rest."

"No!" protested Robert, still trying to get up. "I cannot allow Prince Abram to win."

"It was a tie, a draw," King Louis' deep voice broke in behind Elinore. "Both of you came off the log together."

By this time Robert was on his feet, looking around, reorienting himself. He gazed a moment at the King, absorbing his words. Then he turned to Abram and extended his hand. "Well fought, Prince Abram," he said calmly.

Abram glanced at Robert's hand, but merely nodded. "You were an able opponent."

"Now," said the King, extending his hands toward the doors at either end of the courtyard, through which the men had first entered. "You may return to your rooms to clean up. Dinner will be served in half an hour in the dining room."

Abram gave Elinore a piercing look, then Robert and Abram turned and left. Elinore sighed and leaned against her father. "Thank heaven that is over. I could not bear it if any serious injury . . ."

King Louis put his arm around her as they left the courtyard. "I too am grateful no one was seriously injured."

She nodded. "The next task is mine," she whispered.

At the end of dinner, King Louis stood and conversation quieted. "Princess Elinore will now give you the instructions for your next test." He sat down.

Elinore stood and cleared her throat a couple of times. "As I mentioned before, my test is one of wit and worthiness. Both of you will have three days. Within that time, you must perform a deed that will prove you superior to your opponent in worthiness to have me and the kingdom. The choice of deed will be yours. However, by sundown of the third day you will both return and bring evidence of your deed. It is then the decision will be made. Any questions?"

Robert shook his head slowly, and Abram frowned. "Forgive me, Princess, but who exactly will be judging the merit of our deeds? It seems to me that someone impartial must be judge of this test. And forgive me, Princess, but you are in the middle of this and directly affected, and hardly in a position to judge fairly."

Elinore opened her mouth, then looked at her father. The King nodded. "An accurate assessment," he observed. "Would you both accept me as judge?"

Robert nodded, but Abram looked thoughtful. He glanced from the King to Elinore and back again. "With hesitation," Abram confessed. "Your Majesty is still very closely involved with this issue. Perhaps a neighboring monarch can act as judge?"

"Perhaps this should involve judgement by the people," interjected Robert. "Have them select or choose randomly, say a dozen men to decide the most worthy deed."

Abram snorted and jumped to his feet. "Do you think the common people have sense enough to decide things like this? I would not allow it!"

Robert stood to meet him. "I think they have the most balanced view of all. I would trust their judgement to be fair."

Elinore whispered to her father. King Louis stood and raised his hands. "Gentlemen, Gentlemen," he interrupted. "I think both your ideas are valid. I propose we use both your choices. A neighboring monarch will be chosen at random," he nodded toward Abram. "And you, Prince Abram, can assist me with the choosing. In addition, twelve subjects will be picked at random from a group selected by the people, and you, Robert, may assist me with these lots. Both parties must be unanimous in their choice of winner. Does this meet your approval?"

Robert nodded. Abram hesitated, then he too nodded.

"It is decided then," said the King. "On the morrow at dawn you begin your tasks, and I'll start gathering the names for the judging."

Both men retired to their rooms. Elinore was left sitting at the table with her father. What deeds would the suitors choose? "Good night, Father," she said, rising and giving him a kiss.

"Shall I see you tomorrow?" he asked.

Elinore shrugged. "I think they need me in the morning for another dress fitting, and then I need to exercise Spirit. I shall probably see you again at dinner."

King Louis nodded. "You know where I shall be. Good night."

CHAPTER 6

The Test of Wit and Worthiness

It was late morning when Elinore got away from the dressmakers. She returned to her room to change into her riding clothes. She was about to put on her divided riding skirt, when she spied the clothes Robert of Danforth had loaned her. She had had no opportunity to return them yet, nor would she for a few days. She was suddenly seized with the desire to be unrecognized as she rode. Perhaps she could learn something of what her suitors were planning and doing.

Elinore pulled on the shirt, vest and pants, cinching them in as she had before. She braided up her hair and pinned it to her head. Then padding out into the hall in Robert's thick stockings, she went to the stables. There she found one of the young stable hands, and convinced him to loan her a cap, boots, and coat. Then she put an older plain saddle on Spirit, and rode away from the castle.

After putting Spirit through his workout routine in the neighboring field, she turned him toward the town. It was lunchtime, and she was hungry for some of Georgio's fare. All seemed normal in town. She tied up Spirit at the horsepost on the side of the inn and went inside.

No one paid much attention to her as she slid onto a bench at an empty table. The room was half full of customers, talking and eating. At the table across from her a couple of men were talking, and she could hear occasional comments.

". . . a short bearded man asking questions . . . Danforth . . . family nobility . . ."

"And you said?"

A shrug. "Stablehand apprentice . . . farmer . . . commoner. I don't know."

Elinore sank into thought. A short bearded man, asking about Robert of Danforth's heritage, could only be Prince Abram servant Rala. Abram must be researching out Robert's family. But why? What would it gain him? Elinore sat up straight. Unless Abram was trying to prove Robert's unworthiness to marry her or rule the kingdom based on his birth status. This was not the kind of deed she had had in mind at all.

"Sir?" An inn servant stood at her elbow. "Your order, sir?"

"Oh, I-I'm sorry," Elinore stuttered. "I'll have the house special."

The harried server rushed off, leaving her again to her thoughts. After eating she left Spirit tied up at the inn and strolled over to the marketplace

She wandered around awhile, then as she passed a booth, she heard a couple of women gabbing at the adjacent one. Elinore stopped and pretended to examine the merchandise in front of her.

"Oh yes," said the one behind the booth. "Apparently the trial of skill was a draw. They've been sent out to perform some deed of worthiness."

The woman in front of the booth raised her eyebrows. "Oh? And what are they doing?"

The first woman shrugged. "Who knows what is in that foreigner's mind? Robert, however," and she leaned forward conspiratorily, "is said to be over helping Old Tom Parker bring in his wheat."

"What?!" screeched the second. "What kind of worthiness deed is that?"

"Well, it seems he had promised some time ago to help the old man at harvest time. If you ask me, I think they do more talking than harvesting . . ."

"I think Old Tom has no business planting in the first place after that stroke of his. Which reminds me . . ."

Elinore lost interest as the conversation turned, and she wandered on, thinking. On the one hand, it was admirable of Robert to keep a promise to a peasant, but at a time like this? What kind of royal worthiness would this show to the judges? Did he even really care about her and the kingdom after all?

She stumbled from the marketplace and returned to Spirit's side. As she leaned her face against his warm neck, he nickered softly. It was then she remembered Aunt Lydia's words, that this was only part of the worthiness test, that she would return with the real one.

Elinore's spirit's brightened, and she climbed onto Spirit's back and returned to the castle. She spent the afternoon in the library engrossed in her studies.

The second morning Elinore in disguise again mounted her horse in an attempt to follow her suitors. She found Robert at the north end of the town, sitting on the bank of the stream near where the road passed over a rickety bridge. He appeared to be sketching a picture as he gazed at the bridge. Elinore stayed back behind some bushes, and watched as he got up, walked onto the bridge, stamped on it, and walked across, examining the ground boards. Then he climbed down the bank, and stooping over, crawled underneath to examine the supports. He came out the other side, sloshed across the stream, and sat down on the bank to jot down some more notes. Then he climbed back to the side of the road where his wagon was sitting, and drew out some boards. He measured, cut, pulled them under the bridge, and started hammering them into place.

Elinore withdrew quietly, retrieved Spirit from behind an adjacent cottage, and returned to town. She wandered the market place again, but there was no further gossip of worth.

She was gearing herself mentally to ride the fields again as she led Spirit from behind the Georgio's Inn. Looking up, she saw Prince Abram leaving the magistrate's office with several papers in hand. She backed up quickly and watched him. He stopped at the side of the street, reading one paper with renewed intensity, smiled, wrote some notes on it, then folded the papers and stuffed them into a bag at his hip. He untied his horse, mounted, and rode southward out of town, taking the road that led toward the Black Forest.

Elinore tied Spirit back up, then walked across the road to the magistrate's office. The magistrate's deputies were talking in the front office as she entered.

"The Prince spent over two hours in the office with him," the older one was saying.

"What were they talking about?" asked the younger man.

"I don't know, but the magistrate had me bring several old law books from the back room, you know books about inheritance, royal etiquette, the peasantry, and then some census books and old documents of the King . . ."

The younger man looked up, saw Elinore, and elbowed the older man. He stopped talking, and looked up at her.

"Yes, mister?"

"I-I want to talk to the magistrate," Elinore asked in her deepest voice.

"Can't," he answered. "Magistrate's having his lunch. Come back in an hour." He looked back to his companion as though to dismiss her.

Elinore left, got Spirit, and returned to the castle. She thought she could pretty much figure out what her suitors were up to.

CHAPTER 7

The Invasion

The third morning, just as she was wondering when Aunt Lydia would return, she heard the castle trumpeters calling out an alert. Elinore started running down the corridor toward the Throne Room. As she passed some windows overlooking the courtyard near the front gates, she saw streams of peasants passing through into the courtyard. They were on foot, in wagons, on horses or mules, carrying hastily assembled bundles, but most were women or children.

As she hurried down the final stairway, Elinore ran into her father in the Great Hall. He was listening to the hurried and overlapping reports of two disheveled messengers.

". . . armies on the outskirts of the land. No one could identify their country . . ."

69

"They have taken some of our people prisoner, are looting homes, burning haystacks . . ."

"There is a party of them on their way here now, carrying a white flag. We believe they want to discuss their terms with you."

"But be aware, Your Majesty, they have our land borders fully surrounded."

King Louis' face looked strained. "How did they get into such a position without our border patrols finding them out?"

"Forgive us, Your Highness." The messenger knelt, lowering his head. "They appeared out of camouflage so suddenly. And they have captured several of our patrols."

The King breathed in and out several times. "Thank you," he said. "You may return to your posts." He whirled on his feet, barking orders to his Master-at-Arms, who had appeared on the scene shortly after Elinore did. Other servants arrived with the King's armour and began dressing him as he spoke. The Master-at-Arms left on a run to assemble the army, give further instructions to the castle guards, and alert the reserves.

King Louis turned to his daughter. "Elinore, I need you to organize the peasants that are on the castle grounds. Get them out of the way of the army and out of sight." He turned on his heel and headed toward the stables where his horse was now waiting.

Elinore ran out the main castle entrance and looked out over the milling, crying, confused peasants. She called out to them, but no one heard her over the din. As she looked around for an idea, she saw Prince Abram pushing through the crowds on his horse. He saw her and rode his horse up the steps toward her.

"We are being invaded, Princess!" he announced. "Where is your father?"

Elinore pointed to the other end of the courtyard toward the stables where the soldiers were gathering, the King at their head. Abram kicked his horse and leaped through the crowd in that direction.

Elinore turned back and saw Robert of Danforth now entering the castle gates, driving his wagon loaded with children and elderly peasants. Seeing Elinore on the castle steps, he handed the reins to one of the boys in the wagon, leaped off, and pushed his way to the stairs where she stood.

"I see you know what is happening," he said to her. "What is the plan?"

"I've got to get these people's attention and get them out of the couryard so the army can get through." Her eyes fell on one of the flags flying near the doorway. She ran over to it, lifted it out of its holder, and began waving it madly. Robert grasped the other one. As he joined her again, he threw his head back and let out a long piercing whistle. The din quieted down as astonished peasants noticed the pair on the steps.

"Instructions from her Royal Highness, Princess Elinore!" Robert loudly announced.

Elinore stepped forward. "We must clear the courtyard!" she called out in her strongest voice. This time the people heard. "Take your animals and wagons through those gates at the south end of the courtyard into the Queen's Gardens.

You will enter the castle from there. Those of you on foot, come through these doors. You will be housed in the Throne Room. Now go!"

While Robert guided people at the doorsteps, she retreated through the doors. Surprised and frightened servants met her in the hallway. "Guide these people to the Throne Room," Elinore instructed. "If it fills up, use the Great Hall and Ballroom too. Others will be coming through the South entrance too."

"The South entrance!" one servant woman gasped. "What about the queen's gardens?"

Elinore had already thought of that, but her heart twisted anew inside. She could think of no other place to house the influx of animals and wagons and still get them out of the way of the army. Her mother's prize gardens would be trampled and eaten. "We can replant them," she said, touching the servant's shoulder. "Come. We must get to the South entrance quickly to keep order there."

As they hurried down the halls, Elinore gathered other servants on the way. A few she sent on errands to find food and bedding for the refugees, others she bid follow her. At the South doors she paused and took a deep breath, then pushed them open.

Peasants clustered at the outer gate to the gardens, hesitant to enter. Elinore beckoned them in. "Bring your wagons in to the far side first. We need to make room for others. Tether your animals where they can reach the grass."

She turned to the head gardener at her side, who was wringing his hands. "John, you are in charge of getting things settled how you think best." She grasped his shoulder and looked in his eyes. "It will be all right. Mother would understand." She looked over at the other servants. "We need water for the animals. Fetch all the buckets you can find. The rest of you help John and direct the people to the Throne Room."

When all seemed adequately organized, Elinore hurried back through the castle to discover the status of the King and his army. They had gathered at the castle gates, some inside and the rest without. King Louis himself, mounted on his horse, waited on the drawbridge for an approaching truce party, his flag and armour bearers at his side. Prince Abram on his horse waited nearby. One of the foreign messengers dismounted, approached the King, and knelt at his feet. On arising, he handed the King a parchment scroll.

King Louis unrolled it and scanned it quickly. He glanced up at Elinore a moment, then he read parts of it aloud. "'Here are the terms of our conditions: 1) Your unconditional surrender of the kingdom, 2) or of Princess Elinore. Failure to surrender either one of these means war.'"

Prince Abram had now moved beside the King. "Who sends this, Your Majesty?"

"Some unnamed Lord from a kingdom in the North," snorted King Louis, passing the scroll over to Abram to peruse. "Tell your Lord," he said to the messenger. "We will surrender neither the kingdom nor the princess. He is invited to leave our fair lands, or he will know what war means. I will give him no more than twenty-four hours to leave, or he will be exterminated."

The messenger nodded, returned to his horse, and the party bearing their white flag retreated.

King Louis spoke to his Master-at-Arms. "Send spies out to follow them, discover the strength and location of his main army, and find out who this Lord really is. Meanwhile, I want every able-bodied man in the kingdom armed and sent out with your soldiers to defend the borders of this land. A few castle guards will stay here with the women and children. Send any citizens you find back here for protection."

King Louis beckoned to Prince Abram. "Stay by me, Abram. I may need a messenger." King Louis looked up and spotted Robert of Danforth. He waved him to come to him too. "Come! I would like to confer with both of you, and get your ideas of how we should handle this situation."

The three men moved to a corner just inside the castle wall to talk in private. Elinore watched Prince Abram gesticulating as he talked intently to the king. Robert stood deep in thought beside them.

A servant appeared at Elinore's elbow. "You are needed in the Throne Room, Your Highness. The peasants are distraught."

Elinore turned to follow him, glancing once more over her shoulder toward her father. Robert was trying to speak while Abram waved at him to quiet him, still talking animatedly to the king.

In the Throne room there was chaos. Chilren were crying, two old women were fighting over a piece of bedding, another woman was screaming hysterically while a servant tried to calm her. Families were milling around unable to find places to settle, and servants who brought food or bedding were either mobbed by people trying to get at the supplies, or were wandering around unsure where to take things.

Elinore climbed the steps on which the thrones stood, and clapped her hands to get the people's attention. Most of the people stopped and looked at her.

"My people!" she called. "I need your cooperation." She looked around the room. "First, let's organize this room. Families may settle along the walls and in the middle, leaving space to walk between. I am afraid we only have enough blankets for one per family at present, so please share if you have more. Finally, we have enough food for all, but we may have to feed you in shifts."

She scanned the room again. "Malcolm!" she called, and a servant stepped forward. "Please set up tables for the food and drinking water by the main Throne Room entrance." She looked out again. "I need volunteers to help with various tasks, such as fetching water and bringing in the food, keeping this room as clean as possible, and helping entertain the children. Malcom will be in charge of organizing things, and you will come to him with any problems. Any questions?"

Several peasants shouted questions and concerns. Elinore did her best to answer. "No, I do not know what is going to happen. I do know my father will do his best to protect our land, homes, and families. I do hope we do not need to go to war, but if we do, it will be because there are no other options."

The hysterical woman began screaming again. Elinore left the dais and went over to her. "Please calm down," Elinore pleaded. "and tell me what is wrong."

"My child! I can't find my son!" she sobbed.

Elinore put her arm around her. "Is your child somewhere at the castle?" she asked. The woman nodded. "Have you looked throughout this room?" Again she nodded. "Then come with me. We will look in the Ballroom and the Great Hall. I promise to help you look until your child is found."

Taking the woman by the hand, Elinore led her to the Great Hall. While the woman searched, Elinore calmed and organized the people there, again setting a servant in charge. The child was not found, and Elinore took the tearful woman to the Ballroom.

Within moments a little boy came running up to them, followed by a grandmotherly woman. "Mama, Mama!' he cried joyfully, and the woman picked him up and hugged him tightly, tears rolling down both their cheeks.

Elinore turned away and got to work organizing this room too. Soon she leaned back against a wall in relief, rubbing away the beginnings of a headache at her temples.

"I am hungry," she thought, and went to the kitchens in search of food. It was mayhem there, servants and cooks running in all directions, miraculously avoiding collisions at every turn. Elinore snagged a piece of bread and cheese from a passing tray, then wandered away down quieter halls. Soon she found herself in the stables, empty except for her Spirit. He whinnied when he saw her.

"I'm sorry, Spirit," she sighed, as she leaned her face into his neck. "I can't ride you out today."

Elinore spent the afternoon and evening continuing to settle her people in for an unknown length of stay. A few more peasants were brought to the castle from outlying lands, but most of the army were out patrolling the borders of the land. King Louis still had not returned when Elinore decided to turn in for the night, nor had she heard any news of what was happening beyond the castle. She had heard no word as to the whereabouts of Prince Abram or Robert of Danforth. She fell asleep wondering vaguely how the competition between them would work out, but was very aware of which suitor her heart chose.

CHAPTER 8

The Kidnapping

Elinore awoke with a start when a hand clamped tightly over her mouth. She struggled as a rag was stuffed into her mouth, and when she felt a finger, she bit hard.

"Ow!" said a surprised male voice she vaguely recognized. It cursed softly but vehemently.

Her assailant attempted to pinion her arms, but she got one free and punched him hard in the face. He grunted but didn't loosen his hold on her. She wished she could get her feet free of the bed covers. She tried another tactic, and twisted onto her stomach. He threw the full weight of his body on top of her.

"Umph!" With the gag in her mouth she could barely breathe. One arm was twisted painfully under her and she couldn't quite get it out. With a tremendous effort she pushed up hard, and rolled him off her onto the floor. His head hit the stone with a crack. She managed to free her legs of the sheet, jumped off the bed, and pulled the gag out of her mouth as she ran toward the door.

"Help! Somebody—" she began yelling.

Her attacker was on his feet, grabbed the sheet, and threw it over her. In seconds he had her wrapped tightly in it, though she continued to struggle. Then something hard hit her head, she saw stars, and then all went black.

Elinore awoke slowly out of a gray dream, aware of a painful lump in her middle, and a throbbing headache in the back of her head. She was draped across the back of a horse, and she could tell by the rhythm of the movements that they were going up a hill, winding between trees in the night darkness.

Elinore tried to push herself upright, and discovered that her hands were tied behind her, and her feet were bound as well. The cloth gag had also been replaced. She managed to shift her weight enough to move from the lump she was lying on. She raised her head to see if she could tell where they were going, and got banged in the side of the head by a tree trunk as her horse went around it. More carefully this time, and wincing a little, she managed to make out the shapes of two men, one in front leading the horse, the other behind, who seemed to be on lookout for anyone following them.

After what seemed like hours, and when Elinore thought she could take no more in this position, the man in front stopped. The man in the rear went up to him, and they talked in low whispers. Then the larger of the two pulled

Elinore from the saddle, tossed her across his shoulder like a sack of flour, and stumbled toward a rock wall with a cave-like opening in it. He stooped some, entered into the darkness and dropped her to the ground. The floor of the cave was covered by some sort of animal skins that softened her fall somewhat. Elinore rolled onto her side and groaned in relief.

The smaller man had crept in behind them, and now he lowered his head near Elinore's.

"Welcome to our humble abode, Princess, he said in a very accented voice. His breath rolled over her, strong with some foreign spice. He draped an animal fur across her, which offered warmth to her chilled body. "Sleep, and your questions will be answered in the morning," he told her.

Elinore worked her mouth to try and push the gag free, but it was tied tightly. She tried to speak against the gag.

"Sorry, Princess," he responded. "The gag stays in until Master arrives."

She made herself as comfortable as possible, and at last, convinced that nothing more would happen to her that night, she closed her eyes in sleep.

When the first streaks of dawn peeked in the cave entrance, Elinore awoke, her muscles and lower ribs sore, and her bladder full. She rolled onto her knees, and the movement awoke her foreign, smaller captor.

"Good morning, Princess," he smiled. "It will not be long now."

She looked around, and saw the taller man sleeping in a fur near the entrance. The shorter man kicked him awake. "Check the horses, André."

As the taller man crawled from his skins in the darkness, he grumbled. "You don't have to kick me awake, Rala," he said.

André, Rala! So this was the cave where she had seen them the afternoon of the thunderstorm. But that still didn't explain what these two were doing together, or why they had brought her here.

André had barely left the cave, and Elinore's head was still spinning, when another figure filled the cave entrance. He carried himself with an imposing air, a scimiter hanging at his side. Prince Abram! At sight of him Elinore sat back in surprise.

Prince Abram ducked into the cave, let his eye adjust a moment to the darkness, then approached Elinore and began untying her feet. "Come walk with me," he said, lifting her up by the elbow, her hands still tied behind her. He did not attempt to untie her hands or mouth.

He led her from the cave entrance and into the trees a short distance. "Your country has been attacked," Prince Abram began. Elinore followed him, wondering what this had to do with her abduction. "Your father is left with a terrible decision." Abram paused in his walking to look at her. "He must choose whether to give up his kingdom, or his daughter."

Abram reached a fallen log, and gestured for Elinore to seat herself. She remained standing, gazing at him silently.

"I have been scouting out the enemy," Abram reported. "And they appear strong, though they are not in their home territory. Your people would suffer much loss in trying to push them from your lands." Prince Abram smiled craftily. "But I have a plan to save your father's kingdom and you."

Elinore reached her chin to her shoulder to push the gag away. "Not yet, Princess," Abram stopped her. "The plan is this. Two men appearing to be from your father's army will deliver you to the enemy, to fulfill one of their demands." Elinore's eyes opened wide, and Abram raised a hand as though asking her not to speak yet. "However, you will not be left with them. I will watch them closely, making sure that no harm comes to you. Then, as they are marching home, a band of highway robbers, led by my men, will ambush them and I will rescue you, bringing you home to your dear father." Abram smiled. "In the ambush the leader of the invaders will be slain, the rescue will not be traced to your father, and this war will end. Your father will be grateful to me, and will give me your hand in marriage."

Elinore looked at Abram coldly a moment, then looked away. "Oh also, Princess, you should perhaps know that Robert of Danforth does not have any royal blood in him. His father is not even a land owner in Danforth. It is beneath your dignity to marry him, Princess. I am giving you, how do you say? An out."

Elinore now shot Prince Abram a look with narrowed eyes of venom. How dare he go behind her father's back, kidnap her, and give her up to the enemy! And Robert's lineage was not the point of these tasks, but to find the true inner valor of the suitor who would be king!

Laughing at her expression, Prince Abram reached out to caress her cheek. She pulled her head away. "I am interested to hear your comment on my plan, Princess, and that you are willing to help me. Know that there is no one but the enemy nearby to hear you if you scream. And I can always replace this." He untied the knot fastening her gag, and removed the rag from her mouth.

Elinore retched a couple of times, then worked the muscles of her mouth. She gazed again at Abram coldly. "I have to relieve myself," she said. "Please untie my hands."

Abram looked at her a moment. "I think not, exactly," he said, as though talking to himself. "It would not do to have you run away. But I could tie you to a tree like one hobbles a horse." Abram took a piece of rope from his side, tied one end to her ankle, and the other to a tree. Then he grasped her wrists to untie them.

"If you struggle, I will not leave you a moment's privacy," he told her. "I believe I know your spirit." He finished untying her wrists from behind her, but quickly tied them up again in front of her. "I think that will have to do," he told her. "You have five minutes before I return. Then we will have a little breakfast." With a nod of his head he disappeared from view.

Elinore examined the knot on her ankle and worked at it a moment. It would not come loose. With a sigh, she let it be. Looking around, she made sure that there was a tree between her and the direction Abram had gone. Awkwardly she loosened her garments enough to do what she needed to, and managed to refasten them before Abram returned.

"And now for breakfast!" he said cheerfully, returning through the trees. He handed her some bread and cheese and water, and Elinore was surprised how good it tasted.

As they finished, Abram looked up at the height of the sun rising over the tops of the hills. "It is time," he stated. "I am sorry, but I must replace the gag for now." This time he left her hands tied in front, and they walked back to the cave entrance. There was the horse from last night, saddled and waiting with Rala and André who were now dressed in armour belonging to King Louis' army. Rala bowed deeply.

"All is ready, Your Highness," he said to Prince Abram.

Abram pulled a parchment from inside his shirt and handed it to Rala. It appeared to have the imprint of King Louis' official seal on the outside. Elinore looked up at Prince Abram sharply. He grinned at her. "I borrowed your father's seal briefly. It looks so much more official, don't you agree, Princess?"

She turned her face away from him, but inside she was seething. To use the king's seal without his permission was a capital offense.

Prince Abram lifted Elinore onto the horse sidesaddle, and tied her feet. "Play your part well," he told her. "And we will be able to rescue you. Betray us and you will be left to the mercy of your enemy." Abram grasped her bound hands and kissed them. "Farewell, Princess."

CHAPTER 9

In the Hands of the Invaders

Rala led the horse, while André carried a white flag. Elinore looked briefly over her shoulder at Abram, who watched them leave with a calm smile. Elinore sighed. Perhaps she should have tried to run when her feet were untied. But a part of her had wanted to trust Abram. She hadn't wanted to truly believe that he would go through with this scheme. She determined she would make an escape attempt the next opportunity that presented itself.

Her thoughts then went to her father. Probably by mid morning someone in the castle would discover the scene of struggle in her bedroom, and raise the alarm. Word would be immediately sent to her father patrolling the borders of the land, and he would send out a frantic rescue party. But by then Elinore would be in the hand of the enemy, and possibly on the way to their lands. She was not looking forward to what they had in store for her. But neither was she eager for the end result Prince Abram had planned.

And what of Robert of Danforth? He would join the rescue party the moment he learned of her disappearance, but again, he would probably not be able to track her down until Prince Abram had "rescued" her. Unless . . . Elinore straightened in the saddle. She would do what she could to delay their departure from her land, giving her father and Robert time to devise a rescue, or until she managed to escape herself.

Half an hour later her two escorts stopped the horse briefly to straighten their armour, and lower their visors. Elinore could hear the sounds of men talking and eating in an unseen nearby camp through the trees.

Now was her chance. Leaning over to the right side of her horse with her bound hands, she managed to grasp one of the reins. Jerking it suddenly from Rala's grasp, she pulled the horse's head hard to the right, at the same time she kicked the horse in the withers. Rala cried out, stumbled and fell. The horse backed up, reared, then leaped forward, back the way they had come. Suddenly, the horse jerked sideways, and Elinore nearly toppled off. André had grasped the trailing rein, and now clung firmly to the saddle.

"You are not going to escape me again, Your Highness," he panted. He took out another piece of rope and bound Elinore's hands firmly to the saddle horn, while Rala tied her feet to the stirrups.

Then they led her horse forward once again until they reached a clearing, where the sun felt warm falling on Elinore's shivering shoulders.

"Halt!" cried the voice of one of the soldiers. "What do you want?"

"Audience with your Lord," said André through his closed visor, and waving his white flag and parchment. "We bring a message and a prisoner."

"Obviously," said the soldier, eyeing Princess Elinore. "But I think you shall talk to my Captain first. Follow me."

Rala led the horse after André, and they wound their way through to the center of the camp. Most of the soldiers stopped their activities to stare at the visitors. Elinore thought there was something familiar about the style of their armour, but where their emblems and colors should be, all had been painted black or red.

They stopped in front of a medium sized tent, and their guide spoke to the door guards. "First Lieutenant to speak to the Captain," announced one of the guards.

Elinore noted vaguely that they had announced the men by rank only, without using names.

"Send him in," called a strong deep voice.

First Lieutenant entered the tent briefly, then returned and beckoned to Elinore and her escorts. "All three of you follow me."

Rala loosened Elinore's hands from the saddle horn, untied her feet and pulled her off the horse. She just managed to land on her feet. He grasped her arm tightly and they entered the tent.

The Captain was seated behind a makeshift table, but when he saw Elinore, he arose. "My Lady," he said, bowing his head in her direction.

She nodded her head briefly, watching him carefully.

Captain turned to André. "The parchment," he demanded. André handed it to him, and the Captain sat down again, broke the seal on the parchment, unrolled it, and read it silently. Then he looked up at the two men, still with their visors down over their faces.

"So your King Louis is aware and consents that this Robert of Danforth acts on his behalf in deciding the fate of his kingdom and his daughter?" he asked.

Elinore started at mention of Robert's name, and her hands suddenly felt clammy.

André nodded. "So we are told, Your Honor. We were instructed to obey him and deliver the Princess to you."

Captain gazed at Elinore again. "It seems she is not so willing a participant," he commented. "But no matter. Your king has decided his answer to My Lord's ultimatum, and it is settled. We will leave your lands forthwith." Captain took quill and ink and wrote a message on his own piece of parchment, then rolled it up and sealed it. "Deliver this to your King."

André and Rala bowed and backed out of the tent, leaving Princess Elinore standing before Captain. She heard the two men mount their horse and trot out of camp.

"Now," said Captain, rising again from his chair. "You, Madam, need a little cleaning up before we present you to My Lord." He clapped his hands, and one of the guards from outside the tent door entered. "Fetch the Queen's old nurse to take care of the Princess."

The soldier nodded and left. He returned a few minutes later followed by a bent old woman.

"Follow me," she croaked.

As they left the tent, Elinore looked around her. The soldiers were cleaning up breakfast, sharpening swords, feeding horses. This was not a good time to try to run, especially still bound and gagged. She followed the old nurse into another tent.

"I'll have to untie thee, dearie," squeaked Old Nurse. "But I should not advise thee to try escape just now. Thee would not get far." As she spoke, the old woman's strong fingers untied Elinore's gag and wrist cords.

Old Nurse dug out a big washtub and pulled it to the center of the tent. Then she poked her head out of the tent. "Fetch me hot water!" she screamed. A few minutes later two soldiers lugged in pots of steaming hot water until Old Nurse put a halt to it. Then she turned to Elinore.

"Off with thy clothes, dearie. I'll make sure no one disturbs thee. Then ye shall have fresh linens for thy presenting to My Lord." Then she began to bustle about opening bundles near the sides of the tent, clucking to herself, pulling out something here or there, and ignoring Elinore.

Elinore peeked out the door of the tent. Soldiers were standing in a circle around her tent. She sighed and closed the tent flap again.

She slipped off her dusty nightdress, and eased into the hot water. To her sore muscles the heat was heavenly! She sank deeper into the water until her hair was submerged, sighed and closed her eyes.

"Now there's the soap, dearie," sang Old Nurse, handing it to Elinore.

Elinore washed off the dirt, the gag marks, the rope burns, and the indignity of the night's situation. Finally she felt human again. As she looked up, she caught Old Nurse gazing at her, a tear in her eye.

"That's right, dearie. Thee feels much better. Here's a towel and the clean linens for thee." Old Nurse held up the towel for Elinore, and regretfully she stepped out of the tub and dried off.

The dress laid out for her was of soft lavender silk, and seemed made perfectly for her figure. Old Nurse combed out Elinore's hair, and fastened her long tresses with a lavender silk ribbon.

"Now thee is ready," smiled Old Nurse, looking her over. "Time to go see My Lord."

Elinore followed Old Nurse to the center of the camp, to the largest, grandest tent. The guards at the door pulled their lances back from across the entrance to let them pass, as one of them announced their arrival.

Elinore had time to just glance across the tent toward a figure sitting in a throne-like chair when Old Nurse pulled her to her knees. "Bow before My Lord," she hissed.

Elinore dutifully bowed her head, wondering what kind of Lord this was.

"So this must be her Royal Highness, Princess Elinore," said an authoritative voice, that somehow seemed familiar to her. "You may rise."

Elinore raised her eyes to the figure as she got to her feet, and almost sank to her knees again in surprise.

"Cousin Gilbert!" she gasped. "What are you doing here?"

Cousin Gilbert got up from his throne and hurried over to help Elinore to her feet. "It seems that I'm invading your country," he smiled a little sheepishly. "It was my mother's, your Aunt Lydia's, request that I do so." He nodded toward the corner shadows. Elinore's Aunt Lydia came forward, and embraced her.

"How are you, dear?" she asked, looking her over. "I know this is a little unexpected, but it was all I could come up with at such short notice. Do you think anyone suspects we are behind this?"

Elinore shook her head dazedly, and caught sight of Old Nurse rocking back and forth, her mouth open and eyes shut in silent laughter.

Elinore looked back at Aunt Lydia. "So what were you going to do with me or my father's kingdom once you had them . . . us?" she stammered.

"Why, give them back, of course! At least once we had a pretty good idea of how your suitors showed their colors under pressure," Aunt Lydia replied.

"Which brings me to this letter," Cousin Gilbert looked up from examining the parchment that had arrived with Elinore. "If I know Uncle Louis, he would rather sacrifice his own life or the riches of the kingdom before giving you up into the hands of an unknown tyrant. I can't help but think that this Robert of Danforth turned you in behind your father's back."

Elinore leaped to her feet. "Robert of Danforth did not do this!" she cried vehemently, her fists clenched. "Prince Abram had his servant and a prior suitor named André kidnap me last night from the castle. I spent the night tied up in a cave until dawn, when Abram came and tried to make me guarantee him my hand in marriage." She took a deep breath. "I would bet my life that Robert is not involved with a scheme like this."

She looked over at her cousin. "Gilbert, you need to be warned that Prince Abram is planning an ambush as we leave here, to rescue me and kill the foreign invader."

Gilbert nodded gravely. "Thank you for the warning."

A trumpet sounded outside the tent. "A messenger from King Louis!" announced the herald.

"Quickly," whispered Aunt Lydia, taking rope from Old Nurse's outstretched hands and retying Elinore's wrists. "You must again be the unwilling prisoner of a foreign invader." As she melted into the shadows of the tent and Gilbert sat down, Old Nurse pushed Elinore onto her knees again before My Lord.

The tent door opened, and First Lieutenant escorted in the messenger. They stopped further back than where Elinore was kneeling, and she couldn't see who the messenger was.

"You may speak," My Lord addressed him haughtily.

"I come with a request for parley between Your Lordship and His Majesty King Louis," said the messenger. At his voice, Elinore felt as though her heart had leaped up into her throat.

"And you are . . . ?" asked My Lord imperiously.

"I am Robert of Danforth, one of King Louis' loyal subjects," said the messenger. "I bring a parchment supporting the validity of my claims that this is the King's request."

Elinore smiled slightly to herself. Maybe things would turn out all right after all!

"Robert of Danforth. Robert of Danforth. I've heard that name before," said My Lord. "Ah, yes! You sent a parchment with the delivery of her Highness Princess Elinore this morning!" My Lord rose from his throne, came toward Elinore, lifted her up a little roughly by the elbow, and turned her around to face Robert.

Robert's eyes took in sight of Elinore, from her silk lavender gown, to the rope tying her wrists, then to look askance in her eyes. Elinore looked back at him and shook her head slightly.

My Lord put his arm around Elinore's waist. "She will make a lovely bride for me, don't you think, Robert of Danforth?" He smiled slyly. "I don't think I am adept enough to pass all those tests at Rockridge Island, or whatever. This strategy works much better for me, don't you agree? I get the girl, and when her father dies, I get the kingdom too! So cunning."

Robert's hands were clasping into fists and opening again as he gazed at My Lord. Suddenly his eyes narrowed. "Excuse me, Your Lordship, I may have misunderstood you, but you spoke of a parchment that arrived with the Princess that had my name on it. I do not recall sending such a thing."

"Ah!" laughed My Lord. "That explains why you come to request parlance for the King, when supposedly he has already fulfilled the terms of my ultimatum. Perhaps you are trying to play two sides of this game?"

Robert gritted his teeth. Let me see the letter. Please. Your Lordship."

"By all means," smiled My Lord, sitting down on his throne again. He picked up the parchment and handed it to Robert.

Robert nearly snatched it from My Lord, and read it over quickly. "No, this is definitely not my doing," he said. "The signature is not quite right. I can show you." He looked up at My Lord earnestly, holding out the parchment.

"That won't be necessary," yawned My Lord. "I have decided not to accept the invitation to talk with your king. The offer of his daughter has been made, and I will accept the offer as final." He sat forward a little, and stared at Robert. "You are dismissed," he said firmly.

Robert inclined his head, gazed at Elinore a long moment, then turned and walked out the tent door. Everyone was silent while they listened to the departure of horse's hooves.

CHAPTER 10

The Rescue

"We need to leave at once," Cousin Gilbert stirred himself. "I don't want to allow your original captor much time to set his trap, Elinore, or for your father to take us to open battle. Nurse, make sure Elinore has a travel cloak and her own horse to ride."

After Old Nurse left, and while Aunt Lydia untied Elinore's hands, Gilbert went over to a trunk in the corner of the tent. He opened it, and pulled out a belt with a dagger lengthed scabbord on it. "Try this on, cousin," he said, handing it to Elinore. "I trust you know how to use it?"

Elinore nodded and wrapped the belt around her waist. It had originally been made for a larger person, but several holes had been bored crudely into the leather to make it smaller, and she was able to fasten it on at the right adjustment. She pulled the blade out, tested it against her finger, and whisked it through the air a few times. "It will do," she nodded.

Old Nurse returned with a cloak for Elinore, which when draped across her shoulders, covered the dagger nicely. Old Nurse and Aunt Lydia also put on waist daggers and cloaks, and pulled the hoods over their heads. Elinore followed suit. Meanwhile, Cousin Gilbert was strapping on an armoured breastplate, girding on his sword, and covering all with his own cloak. He looked up at the women. "Ready?" he asked. They nodded. "Then we go," he announced.

Outside the tent, My Lord snapped his fingers to his door guards. "Our horses and fifteen men, including two archers, north of camp," he ordered. They scrambled in different directions. By the time Gilbert and the women had reached the north end, their saddled horses and fifteen armed men, including Captain and First Lieutenant, were waiting for them.

My Lord conferred with Captain a minute, who mumbled, "Take the western route," nodded, then called to his men. "Break camp! We leave in half an hour!" There was scrambling of men all around them, tents were being pulled down, fires stamped out, and gear thrown into packs.

My Lord turned to First Lieutenant. "We go over the pass northward, alert for ambush. If spotted, Robert of Danforth and Prince Abram are not to be killed, understand?" Lieutenant nodded. "Inform your men."

My Lord helped Elinore onto her horse. "We need to give the illusion of your being tied, yet leave you free to defend yourself." He held the rope in his hands.

Elinore smiled, and held out her wrists. "Wrap it loosely, about a hand width apart," she instructed. "Then fasten the ends." When he was done, she twisted one wrist around the loops twice, and the rope crossed between the wrists, giving the appearance of being tightly tied. "I used to twist Celia's yarn this way when we were winding it," she explained with a laugh.

When everyone was ready, My Lord nodded his head toward First Lieutenant. Lieutenant led out in front with half of the soldiers escorting My Lord and the women, then the rest of the men followed out of sight behind them. Soon the road they were on wound into the trees of the Black Forest.

The company was quiet, and Elinore could hear the forest sounds around them, twitters of occasional birds and squirrels, the creaking of trees. The clopping of hooves soon was muffled by pine needles on the road, and the occasional snort or lip blowing of the horses sounded loud in the forest.

As the road narrowed and began winding up into the true mountains, the silence deepened, and Elinore was suddenly nervous. She started at the sounds of twigs breaking, or the scurrying of animal feet.

Suddenly she heard a barely audible whish, and something went past her ear, narrowly missing My Lord, and struck First Lieutenant in the back of the left shoulder. He slumped over his horse's neck, and the company halted in confusion.

Then a figure dropped out of a tree before them, arrow poised in his bow, pointed toward My Lord's heart. Another figure came out of the bushes behind them, armed with a crossbow. It was Rala in front and André in back, dressed as woodland bandits. As she watched, a dozen similarly dressed men, variously armed with bows, clubs and flat swords, came out of the trees and surrounded the traveling party.

"Give us all your gold," demanded Rala. "Or we shoot your Lord where he sits."

Only My Lord and the Queen had any coins with them, and these they tossed to the ground.

"Jewelry too," commanded Rala. The Queen gave them a bracelet and necklace, but that too was all.

Rala stamped his foot. "What a paltry collection!" he raged. "Have you nothing else of worth?" Then a smile crept along his face. "Wait, I see you have a prisoner in the form of a lovely young lady! I think we will relieve you of this burden. She will make a fine prize worth our work today." The bandit men cheered.

"No!" began My Lord, but more arrows pointed directly at him.

André put down his crossbow, and stepped forward, grinning. As he passed by Old Nurse's mount, she kicked her horse forward into him, knocking him down. Instantly, three arrows hit Old Nurse, one in the arm, one in the chest, and one in the back. She fell from her horse limply. André got to his feet again, no longer smiling.

"I recommend that no one else interfere," suggested Rala coldly. "Or you too will taste of our arrow pricks."

André grasped the reins of Elinore's horse and began pulling it from the center of the group. Taking a risk that they would not shoot her, Elinore swung back her foot and kicked him in the jaw, hard. He staggered backward, still holding the reins, jerking the horse forward. The rope around Elinore's hands, tangled in the saddle horn, kept her from falling off. André, now furious, grasped Elinore roughly around the waist and jerked her off the horse, tearing her hands free of the saddle horn. Still unable to loose her bands, she wriggled and kicked until two more bandits came to André's aid. One grabbed her legs, and another her hair, until they pinned her face down on the forest floor beside the road. André sat on her back.

"You always showed some spirit, madamoiselle," puffed André above her.

Elinore didn't reply, for just then the sound of horse hooves came up the road, then slowed and stopped.

"What have we here?" said a voice, liltingly accented. Elinore felt the fury rise in her at Prince Abram's voice. "May I be of some assistance?"

"Go back where you came from, Sir," said Rala's voice. "Or perhaps you too would care to make a financial donation to our cause?"

"I do not think so," drawled Prince Abram.

Elinore heard the twang of one arrow, then several others, then there was shouting, horses neighing and stomping, and the clash of sword against sword. Suddenly the weight of André was knocked off her body, and she found she was able to rise. She twisted her wrists back around the rope and freed her hands from the loop. Quickly she pulled the dagger from her waist and turned to face the battle. A hand grasped her left arm firmly and yanked her backward into the trees. She slashed behind her with the dagger, and another hand caught her right arm. She twisted around and came face to face with . . . Robert of Danforth!

"Shhh!" he commanded, and pulled her behind some bushes and to the ground. "Stay here! You'll be safer. I've got to go help Prince Abram."

"Let me go!" she demanded. "I've got to go help Cousin Gilbert!"

He stopped dead still while he stared at her. "Cousin Gilbert?" he asked.

She took a deep breath. "It's a long story. Gilbert is the invading Lord I'm traveling with, the son of Queen Lydia of Adonia. They are not really trying to invade our land. Abram had me kidnapped and turned over to the invading Lord, so he could ambush them and rescue me and return me to my father and be given my hand in marriage. That's why we've got to stop Abram from killing my cousin Gilbert!" She was panting by the end of her speech.

Robert rose to his feet, a slow smile spreading on his face. "I see. Stop Abram from killing Lord Gilbert," he nodded. "I can do that." He turned on his heel and ran toward the battle.

Elinore followed him. At the edge of the forest by the road she saw André lying motionless where he had been thrown off of her. Lord Gilbert's soldiers were battling the bandits that were armed with swords and clubs; the bandit bowmen had been killed. Elinore could see Prince Abram sword fighting with Lord Gilbert. Gilbert's left arm was bleeding, but despite his weight was dodging Abram's thrusts pretty well. However, Abram was gradually moving him toward the stream on the far side of the road. And Robert was approaching carefully behind Abram.

Suddenly Lord Gilbert's foot slipped on the bank of the stream, and he went down into the water on his left side. Almost immediately Prince Abram leaped down beside him, his sword arm raised for the final blow. But before he could deliver it, Robert jumped down behind him, and whacked him hard on the head with the broadside of his sword. Prince Abram crumpled onto the bank. Robert of Danforth extended his hand to help Lord Gilbert out of the stream.

"Thank you," Lord Gilbert panted, climbing to his feet. "If you hadn't been there . . ." He peered closer at Robert. "But you're Robert of Danforth! What are you doing here, and why are you helping me?"

Robert put his hand up as though to stop him. "I understand that you are Gilbert, Princess Elinore's cousin?"

"Yes," Lord Gilbert wheezed. "I mean . . . ahem. You seem to have caught me by surprise."

"So am I to understand that you are not really trying to marry Princess Elinore?" Robert persisted.

"No," said Gilbert, shaking his head.

"Does that mean you are also not really invading King Louis' kingdom?" Robert demanded.

"Yes, that is right," sighed Lord Gilbert.

Robert stood still, thinking.

"Does that mean you did not really deliver Elinore to me?" asked Gilbert.

"I did not!" Robert asserted. "I understand that it was Prince Abram that had her kidnapped to deliver her to you."

Gilbert nodded. "Shall we get out of the stream, then?" he said, laying his hand on Robert's arm.

Elinore looked around the battle scene again. Most of the bandits had been subdued or slain. Lieutenant was alive and giving orders, and it appeared that someone had removed the arrow from his back. André was starting to stir, but Rala appeared to be dead. At the side of the road Queen Lydia was seated on the ground, Old Nurse lying on her side, arrow still in her back, her head resting in Lydia's lap. The queen was stroking Nurse's face, talking to her softly. Elinore approached and knelt beside them. Nurse twitched slightly.

"How is she?" Elinore asked gently.

Aunt Lydia raised her tear streaked face. "I did not plan this kind of sacrifice," she whispered.

Elinore touched Old Nurse's shoulder. "Thank you for making me feel welcome and respected again when I arrived at your camp this morning," Elinore told her.

Nurse let out a sigh of air and seemed to relax. Queen Lydia held Old Nurse's body to her and rocked her, eyes closed, crying silently. Elinore stood and left them.

Lord Gilbert was calling out orders. The horses were being loaded with the wounded, while the bodies were being dragged to the side of the road. Gilbert glanced up and caught sight of Elinore.

He pointed his chin toward Prince Abram. "I suppose we have to take Prince Abram back to your father alive," he commented drily. "Seems a shame not to just kill him and be done with him." He glanced sideways at Elinore.

Elinore gazed at Abram, who was now awake and sitting up, resting his head in his bound hands, arms resting on his bound legs, looking a little ill. A soldier was standing alert guard over him. She glanced at André similarly bound and guarded, but he didn't seem to have the same headache, just looked disgruntled.

"No," she finally responded. "I am still very angry at him for abducting me, but I don't think he should die."

Abram raised his head to gaze at Lord Gilbert. "I am here to rescue the princess," he cried out. "The King, her father, will not let you get away with this!" Abram saw Elinore, and nodded his head in Robert of Danforth's direction. "There is the man who is the traitor to the King. He attacked me while I was battling the invading warlord. It is apparent they are in league together. He must be punished! Release me, Elinore!"

Elinore shook her head.

Abram looked at her and smiled confidently. "I would make a good king and husband for you, princess," he said. "You would reconsider?"

She shuddered. "Never!" she said firmly.

Finally horses were brought to Princess Elinore and Queen Lydia. Suddenly Robert was beside her, holding the horse steady for her and offering his knee to boost her up.

"Thank you, Robert of Danforth," was all she could think of to say.

The ride back to the castle felt long. Robert rode by her side, but as she was not talkative, he said very little. Elinore was dozing in the saddle and the sun had set by the time they arrived. King Louis ran down the front steps to greet them and help Elinore from the saddle. He held her long and hard. Then the castle staff escorted the visitors to their quarters, and by Celia's side Elinore stumbled to her room. A light meal was waiting for her in front of a warm fire in the grate. Elinore ate a few bites, fell into her newly cleaned bed, and fell fast asleep.

CHAPTER 11

The Winner

Elinore slept late the next morning. When she finally arose, she ate the food Celia had left in her room, dressed, and went to find her father. He was in the Throne Room, holding audience with some of the peasants, mainly working out reimbursements for damaged property. Other servants were cleaning up the room from the vestiges of having housed people until the previous night.

When King Louis saw Elinore, he called a recess, and drew her into a small room behind the Throne Room where they could visit together more privately.

"How are you doing, daughter?" he asked kindly as she seated herself.

She gazed downward while fidgeting with her hands and shrugged. Then she looked up at her father. "What happened to Prince Abram?" she asked.

"The neighboring monarch judge and the twelve jury of the people have ruled against him; he did not win the contest. He is in the prison tower at the moment, as is André. Abram will say nothing, but André has confessed the details of the plot regarding your kidnapping, in exchange for his life." King Louis sighed. "What do you think we ought to do with the two of them?"

She shuddered. "Banish them, I don't care. I never want to see either one of them again!" she said vehemently.

"So I assume it is safe to say that you do not desire to marry Prince Abram?" he smiled.

She shook her head sharply. "I don't want to think about marriage ever again! I'm done with this whole suitor thing."

King Louis' smile vanished. "What should I tell Robert of Danforth?" he asked quietly.

Elinore froze and stared at her hands a long time. "I need some time," she whispered.

He nodded. Then standing, he laid his hand on her shoulder, gave it a squeeze, and returned to the peasants waiting for him in the Throne Room.

Elinore wandered the castle aimlessly for a while. Her feet found their way toward the stables and Spirit's stall. She snuggled against Spirit awhile, drinking in his warmth and horse smell. He nickered and blew on her neck. Almost before she knew it, she had bridled and saddled him, swung onto his back, and loped out through the castle gates, ignoring the guard at the gate calling to her to come back.

She loped Spirit until he was lathered by sweat. Then she sat back while he trotted, then walked. Gradually she became aware that she was in a meadow with a haystack in it. On the far side was a barn that looked familiar. She took the road past it around a bend, and nestled among some trees was a cottage that looked homey and welcoming. She reigned in her horse and stared at it, trying to remember why it looked familiar.

A voice spoke at her ear. "No one is home right now, My Lady. What do you seek?"

She turned swiftly in her saddle, and riding on a horse she had not heard approach sat Robert of Danforth. His horse was breathing hard from a more recent run than hers.

"I did not hear you approach," she said. "Why did you follow me?"

He cocked his head to one side and looked at her. "I did not want some bandit to hijack you again," he said, his tone serious.

Elinore shuddered, glanced in the direction of the Black Forest, and looked at the cottage again. Then she turned her horse's head back in the direction of the castle and started him walking. Robert followed. They went in silence for several minutes.

"I'm tired of this Test and Suitor business," she stated.

"So your father told me," Robert said.

"I don't care if I never get married," she said.

"Whatever makes you happy," he responded.

"I'm sick of politics, being wanted for just my money, and having to solve other people's problems," she said.

"I don't blame you," said he.

"I may abdicate the kingdom and become a hermit," she said.

"I know a nice little cottage that has few neighbors and is self sustaining," he said.

"I don't want any strings attached to live there," she responded.

"It is yours as a gift, no strings attached," he told her. "I will move as far away as you desire, and only visit when you ask me to, even if it is never."

A tiny smile played on Elinore's lips. "I might need help bringing in the wheat, and chopping enough wood for the winter fuel," said she.

"I know someone who could do that for you," he said, smiling gently back.

"And if the roof should leak, I would need someone to repair it," she said.

"Not a problem," he said.

She was silent again awhile. "I think the winter evenings will be long and lonely without some company," she said. "Do you know anyone who likes to read, tell stories, or sing?"

"Maybe even dance a little," he nodded.

She smiled. "It would be nice to have a friend with whom to talk ideas, and who doesn't think women are only to look pretty, obey their husbands and provide personal services."

He was silent a moment. "I like 'pretty' with a good mind and an indomitable spirit," he said quietly.

She was silent awhile. "Why didn't you take the Test of Rimrock Island before now, Robert of Danforth?" she looked at him accusingly.

He looked sheepish. "I didn't want to get in the way of your happiness," he confessed.

She sighed. "I don't think I can give up my career after all, Robert," she said.

"You will still need a place to get away," he told her. "The cottage is still available, as is the company . . . and the friendship."

"I don't suppose you could stay on the premises on a constant basis, could you?" she asked.

"People would talk if anything looked improper," he said. "I'm afraid I could only do that under the institution of marriage."

She pondered that for a moment. "Well then, I guess there is no other option," she said. "We'll just have to get married."

"If that is what you really want, Princess Elinore," he said quietly, seriously.

She paused, then nodded. "You'll have to just call me 'Elinore' then," she smiled.

"Hm. Will I then be just Robert?" he asked.

"You will be to me," she answered. "But to our people you will be King Robert, true winner of the Test of Rimrock Island, rescuer of Queen Elinore . . . and my best friend." At that she stopped her horse, reached across to Robert to pull him close, and kissed him.

And he kissed her tenderly, then passionately back.

Edwards Brothers Malloy
Oxnard, CA USA
July 19, 2013